W9-BVF-779

* * * *

The Callaway family's roots grow deep in the Texas soil. For generations, they worked hard to make certain the family and the land flourished.

Three brothers—Cole, Cameron and Cody—expanded and consolidated the family holdings, fighting for what they believed in, risking everything they had—including their lives—to protect those they loved.

Now it is up to the next generation to put their strong family traits to the test.

Cole's sons, Clint and Cade, and Cameron's son, Matt, are prepared to make a stand for what they believe in, defying anyone to take away what they hold closest to their hearts.

This is the story of three more Callaway men bound to the land they call home, prepared to do battle for the women they love....

ANNETTE BROADRICK

is a native of Texas, currently residing in the hill country of central Texas. Fascinated by the complexities found in all relationships, she continues to write about life and love, joy and fulfillment, and the bountiful gifts that are bestowed upon us as we travel along life's path.

Sons of Texas: Rogues and Ranchers is Annette Broadrick's forty-fifth novel.

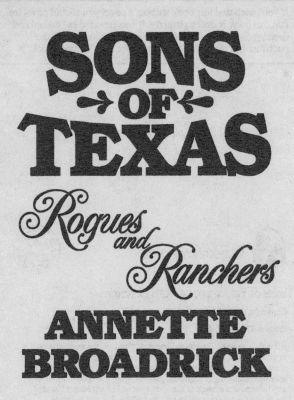

SONS
→OF←
TEXAS

Rogues and Ranchers

ANNETTE
BROADRICK

Silhouette Books

Published by Silhouette Books

America's Publisher of Contemporary Romance

SILHOUETTE BOOKS

SONS OF TEXAS: ROGUES AND RANCHERS

Copyright © 1996 by Annette Broadrick

ISBN 0-373-48336-8

I WISH TO DEDICATE THIS NOVEL ABOUT A
FAMILY TO ALL THE MEMBERS OF MY
FAMILY—WHETHER OUR BOND IS BLOOD
OR SPIRIT EACH OF YOU IS VERY
PRECIOUS TO ME

CALLAWAY FAMILY TREE

Letitia ——— Grant m. Virginia Dupree

Cole ① m. Allison Alvarez

Andrea Galway (d) m. **Cameron**

Janine Talbot m. ②

Cody ③ m. Carina Ramirez

Tony ④ m. Christina O'Reilly

Katie

Trisha

Travis (a)

Matt (a) ⑤ m. Jill Anderson | div. Steve Anderson

Emma

Sherry Lynn

Clay

Kerry

Denise

Clint ⑤ m. Gabrielle Rousseau
≈

Cade ⑤ m. Candy Monroe

Jason Cole   Jacob Carl   Jon Calhoun

SONS OF TEXAS:

1.—*Love Texas Style!*
2.—*Courtship Texas Style!*
3.—*Marriage Texas Style!*
4.—*Temptation Texas Style!*
5.—*Sons of Texas: Rogues and Ranchers*

Key:
≈ = twins
d = deceased
a = adopted

Prologue

The angelic beings—Aurora, Ariel and Aramis—hovered together, discussing their concerns regarding their earthly charges, waiting for the meeting to be called to order.

The three guardians settled themselves into one of the angelic rows and focused their attention on their sovereign leader with some trepidation.

The truth was that the three of them were having some difficulty in their collective roles as guides and counselors. Thankfully they had proven their worth in the protection part of their duties, otherwise the three rather reckless men they had been assigned would not still be on the earthly plane.

However, their guidance skills were being tested to the utmost, for it was time for each of the men to take the next step in their evolutionary growth. Yes. It was time for them to form the lasting relationship with the mates that would help them increase their capacity to give and accept love.

If only human beings could understand the importance of—and their vital need for—that beautifully refined energy known as love. How much simpler the position of guide and protector would be.

Their sovereign leader spoke, immediately calming their minds and soothing their hearts.

"I've called this meeting at your request," He said gently. "I understand that you wish some assistance."

Aurora spoke up. "Oh, yes, Your Holiness, if you would be so kind."

"How may I help?"

Aurora glanced at Ariel and Aramis for permission to speak for all of them. They both nodded.

"Well, sir, as you know, Ariel and I were assigned to Clint and Cade Callaway when they were born thirty-four years ago. It has been a very rewarding assignment. They were born into a very loving family who taught them much of what they needed to know, which made our jobs a lot easier."

"I'm pleased to hear that."

"Yes, sir. The thing is . . . I mean, everything has gone very well for them as they each developed their own skills and interests, but now that it is time for them to commit their lives to another person, we seem to have lost all influence over them.''

"I see.''

Nothing more was said for several moments. Then their leader turned to Aramis. "Is your story a similar one?''

"Well, sir. It is and it isn't."

"Perhaps you could be a little more specific?''

"Well, Matthew's early childhood was far from loving, sir. He never knew his father and his mother was involved in debilitating addictions that rendered her incapable of looking after him. My protective skills were honed tremendously in order to keep him from harm until he was able to look after himself.''

"Obviously you did a good job. He's still on the planet.''

"Thank you, sir. By the time he was nine, Matthew was capable of taking care of himself to a rather alarming degree, I'm afraid. He was getting into all kinds of trouble with the law.''

"Hmm.''

"His adoptive father, Cameron Callaway, is a lawyer who donates a great deal of his time to representing those who are unable to afford legal representation. I 'arranged' to have Cameron appointed by the juvenile court to represent Matthew.''

"A fortuitous pairing, indeed.''

"It was splendid, sir, perfectly splendid. There was all sorts of rejoicing in our realms when Cameron eventually requested custody of the young lad and later adopted him." His smile faltered. "Although Matthew was given a fine example of the healing powers of love, he is now thirty-six years old and shows no sign of wanting to have a loving, permanent relationship in order to establish a family unit."

"Certainly an understandable attitude given his relationship with his mother."

"Yes, sir. He's had a great deal to overcome, I know. However, it is his destiny to heal completely and to have the pleasure of fathering, and loving, children of his own."

"What I am hearing from each of you is an unspoken request for a touch of heavenly intervention to help these three men along their paths."

"If you deem proper, of course," the three guardians reverently intoned.

After another, rather lengthy pause, their sovereign nodded. "Do what you must to ensure the necessary growth in these three men . . . being as gentle as possible, of course."

With beaming smiles, the three nodded their heads vigorously and echoed, "Of course, Your Holiness. Of course."

PART I
Clint

Chapter 1

She had been at her desk working almost an hour that particular Monday in October when her phone rang.

"Agent Rousseau," she answered absently, still scanning memos that had been left on her desk during the three weeks she'd been away on assignment.

"Gabrielle, glad to have you back," Ken Russell said in response. "You did a fine job on that last case you handled. The powers that be couldn't be happier."

"Glad to hear it, sir," she replied. That was high praise from the boss-man, himself.

"I've got something new to discuss with you, if you have a few minutes," he went on, as though, having gotten through the formalities he could get on with the real purpose of the call.

"I'll be right there," she said and hung up. She sighed, looking at her desk. She had a hunch she wasn't going to have time to do any more straightening of the premises.

Then again, she hadn't joined the agency five years ago to shuffle papers. She loved her job, even though it wasn't an officially recognized one. She, along with the other agents, was listed as an employee of a large government firm. No one outside the agency knew she worked in the intelligence branch of government as a covert operative.

Gabrielle brushed the wrinkles from her navy blue skirt, adjusted her matching jacket and brushed back nonexistent wisps of her dark hair before she walked down the hallway to the office of the agent-in-charge.

She tapped on the door and after hearing Ken's voice, she opened the door and stepped into the room.

There were two men in the room. Ken sat behind the government-issued desk that took up a fair share of the room. Ken had been an agent for more than twenty years. Those years were apparent on his face and in the gray hair he wore clipped short.

The other man had his back to the room. He stood with his hands in his pants pockets staring out the window as though he had nothing to do with what was going on in the room.

Gabrielle didn't have to see the man's face to recognize the tall, broad-shouldered, dark-haired figure standing there.

Clint Callaway, the lone wolf of the department, was making one of his rare appearances.

Clint was a law unto himself. He had a formidable reputation in the business. She'd heard tales about him as soon as she joined the agency—how he preferred working alone, how he followed a lead as if he were a hungry wolf tracking its prey, how relentless he was.

Gabrielle knew that he was thirty-four years old and had never married. Someone once mentioned that he was originally from Texas but had worked out of Washington, D.C. for years.

She also knew that his dark good looks caused most women to give him more than a second glance.

He never seemed to notice.

The fact that he was there in Ken's office at this particular time made her uneasy, although she covered her feelings with her usual calm.

Ignoring the man at the window, she looked at Ken and asked, "You wanted to see me?"

"Sit down, Gabrielle. I need to bring you up-to-date on a case." As though aware of his brusqueness, he nodded toward Clint. "You and Clint know each other, I presume?"

She glanced toward the window and saw that Clint had turned and was staring at her, his black-eyed gaze boring through her like a laser. He gave her a brief nod without speaking.

"Yes," she replied, sitting in the chair Ken had indicated to her.

"Clint's been working on something for several months now and it looks as though we've made an identification of sorts. As you know, Clint prefers working solo but I believe I've convinced him that with the right partner he could get the necessary evidence we need to sew this one up in a matter of days."

He paused as though expecting her to comment. When she didn't, he continued. "I believe by utilizing your talents we can bring this case to a speedy and satisfying conclusion."

Gabrielle glanced at Clint, who was facing her with his arms crossed, studying her. She found his calm gaze unnerving and annoying. "My talents, sir?" she repeated, speaking pointedly to Ken and doing her utmost to ignore the enigmatic man whose eyes seemed to be taking in the most minute details regarding her appearance... and condemning them.

"Mmm," Ken replied, flipping through a file on his desk. Only then did she realize that he had her personnel file in front of him. "It says here that you were involved with a drama club in college and that you sang with different dance bands and combos that formed on campus during those years.''

"That's correct,'' she replied slowly, wondering what possible significance her college hobbies could have on her present occupation.

"Good. Then you won't have any trouble with what we've decided to do." He glanced at Clint. "Why don't you explain what's going on?''

Clint straightened and once more put his hands into his pockets.

"In the first place," he said in a deep baritone, "I don't necessarily agree with Ken that having you on the case will move it along any faster. I already have surveillance men set up with all the court orders approving wire tapping on this guy. I think that, sooner or later, we'll get what we need, but I've been overruled on this one.''

It was obvious that he wasn't pleased by the situation.

Gabrielle shifted in her chair, uncrossing, then recrossing her legs. "What has this man done?''

Clint walked over and sat down in the chair beside her, his legs outstretched. The position looked relaxed and casual. The man did not.

"I've been following a money laundering trail for months. Finally, just last week, I was able to narrow down the suspects to one man. Raphael Romero. What he's done is brilliant. He's probably been doing this for years.

"Romero's an illusionist, which gives him reason to travel around the world performing in various cities. He uses his travels to redistribute cash from one country to another. It's a case of now you see it, now you don't. He's very good at what he does, both onstage and off. Because of his movements, he's hard to keep track of, but I've got a chance to nail him now that he's here in the States. He's booked into an extended engagement in Vegas."

"Which is where you come in," Ken added, nodding toward Gabrielle.

"Me? Why?"

"You're going to become part of the revue that plays at the casino where he's performing. That will give you a reason to be backstage picking up any information that might become available. We'll need you to get to know the people he works with, find out more about him through them, learn his daily routine, who he sleeps with, that sort of thing. We're going to find the weak link in his organization and nail him."

She stared at Ken in dismay. "You want me to become a show girl?"

Both men looked at her as though surprised by her reaction, then visually inspected her from the top of her head to the tip of her toes.

She already knew what they saw. She certainly didn't have the measurements that added up to a show girl. First of all, she wasn't tall enough. She was barely five inches over five feet. Secondly, she was too slender in all the wrong places to cause anyone to look at her twice.

"I'm not certain I could convince anyone that I belonged on a Las Vegas runway," she murmured, feeling the heat of a blush flow over her face at their continued analytical stares.

Gabrielle took pride in the fact that she had won her present position through the use of her intelligence, her perseverance, and her sheer determination to gain an education. She'd never attempted to use her physical appearance in any way to get ahead.

A good thing, she thought wryly. *Otherwise, she certainly wouldn't have gotten very far.*

"She's got a point," Clint said in his usual, blunt manner.

"Don't worry," Ken replied. "When Sylvia gets through with her, her own mother won't recognize her." He paused, clearing his throat. "Besides, she's the only one available at the moment."

Clint rubbed his chin thoughtfully, studying Gabrielle with a detachment usually reserved for a mannequin, not a human being.

"It can't be helped, I suppose," he finally said, causing a flash of indignation to sweep over her at his resigned tone of voice.

She wasn't *that* bad, she wanted to say. Instead she focused her gaze on Ken and waited for further instruction.

Ken leaned back in his chair, twirling a pencil between his fingers. "Besides, you won't actually be one of the chorus girls. You'll be a solo act. We've got one of our informants willing to help us out on this deal. Sylvia's going to show you her old routine, give you tips on applying stage makeup, that sort of thing. You'll be working with Howard, her piano player. They fully understand what's at stake here and are willing to do everything in their power to make the operation a success."

Clint stood and asked, "How soon can we move on this thing?" He sounded impatient.

"Today's Monday," Ken said after looking at his desk calendar. "Gabrielle can work with Sylvia and Howard for the next three days or so. That will allow the two of you to fly to Vegas in time for the weekend performances."

Gabrielle stood and looked at Clint. "If I'm supposed to be a singer, who are you?"

Clint gave her a sardonic look. "Me? I'll be your lover, of course. A very protective, possessive lover. You won't ever be out of my sight, Ms. Rousseau, you may rest assured of that."

The early-morning meeting with Ken and Clint was just the beginning of a very hectic day for Gabrielle. She hurriedly cleared her desk, then took a cab to the address Ken had given her, where she would meet Sylvia and Howard and begin rehearsing her newest role.

As soon as she met Sylvia Sandoval, Gabrielle knew she was in big trouble. Sylvia was a tall, buxom blonde who looked a little worn around the edges. She answered the door with a drink in one hand and a cigarette in the other. After looking Gabrielle up and down, she asked, "You from the IRS or something?"

"No. Ken Russell sent me. He said that you and Howard would be working with me for the next few days."

Sylvia burst into good-natured laughter and waved her inside the large, messy apartment. "Oh, honey! Is our work going to be cut out for us! You look more like you should be singing in a church choir than in a Vegas revue!"

Gabrielle discarded all the many things that came to mind as a retort, determined to keep her cool and prove to all of them that she was a professional.

She could handle this assignment.

She'd show them all.

"As a matter of fact, I *have* sung in a church choir," she replied evenly.

"Howard, come look at our new songbird, will ya?"

Where Sylvia was large and overblown, Howard was a thin man with a receding hairline and an accountantlike myopic stare through thick glasses.

"Pleased to meet you," he said shyly, shaking her hand.

"C'mon, honey," Sylvia said in her brash voice. "We've got a great deal to cover in a very short while. Time's a' wasting." She led the way into another room where a piano sat in one corner as if it were a pet bear waiting to perform.

By nine o'clock that evening, when Gabrielle finally reached her small apartment, she felt as though she'd been run over by a Mack truck.

Sylvia had kept a running commentary going throughout the day while she decided what to do with Gabrielle's hair, showed her how to skillfully apply stage makeup, measured her for the costumes to be made for her and gave her the music she was supposed to learn in the next few days.

More than half asleep on her feet, Gabrielle removed her clothes and found a cotton nightgown to put on before falling into bed. She'd learned early in her career to deal with the danger inherent in her job description, but she'd never figured on baring her body to and sharing her less-than-spectacular voice with an audience used to talented, stunningly attractive people.

Her sleep that night was disturbed by restless dreams of finding herself in front of an audience wearing no clothes, or opening her mouth to sing and nothing coming out, or of a sea of faces laughing at her, jeering at her, pointing fingers at her.

She woke up in a cold sweat to discover it was only a little past two o'clock in the morning. She was to meet Sylvia and Howard at nine to start rehearsing the music. The thought terrified her. She wasn't certain she would ever have a peaceful night's sleep until this assignment was over.

The face staring at her in the mirror the next morning startled her into full wakefulness. She hadn't removed the makeup from the night before, so that her eyes were heavily shaded and outlined and her cheeks were prominent in her face.

Her hair was another shock. Sylvia had suggested that they highlight her hair with blond streaks. The stylist had trimmed and shaped her hair into a tousled look that was deceptively sophisticated. Somehow her green eyes appeared to be larger than normal, their color intensified. Even her mouth looked fuller. She'd never noticed before how her bottom lip looked almost pouty.

Unfortunately there was little that could be done with her body to make it look more voluptuous, although the seamstress hadn't seemed to be bothered by her lack of feminine dimensions.

None of that could be helped now. She had to get ready for another long day of learning all the ins and outs of being a performer. She'd always taken pride in carrying out her assignments with efficiency. Now she was going to have to add a certain flair, as well.

As she stood under the shower, Gabrielle knew that somehow she would be playing the toughest role of her career. She could only hope it wouldn't last long.

Chapter 2

Clint woke up in a foul mood Thursday morning. Today was the day he would be flying to Las Vegas, with agent Rousseau in tow.

He'd argued himself hoarse trying to convince Ken that he could handle this assignment without help. But the one thing he couldn't dispute was the fact that having a woman backstage would facilitate their operation considerably.

After grudgingly accepting the fact that he wasn't going to win that particular argument, he was next confronted with Ken's choice of Gabrielle Rousseau as his partner.

He'd taken an instant dislike to the woman as soon as he'd met her when she'd first been hired. Her calm, unruffled composure irritated the hell out of him. Nothing seemed to faze her. She never raised her voice, but like a true government robot, performed her duties with meticulous accuracy. Other agents who worked with her praised her to the skies, saying she was innovative, creative and a hell of a backup in tight situations.

He'd made it a point to avoid this paragon of virtue for years. Now, unfortunately, he was stuck with her.

Miss Uptight-Agent-By-Rote Rousseau might discover that working with him was an entirely different matter from what she was used to. By the time they got through this particular assignment, she'd be begging Ken to return her to more formal duties in the department.

He smiled at the thought. He was going to enjoy watching the woman make a complete fool of herself onstage.

Clint gave the cabdriver the address for Gabrielle's apartment, then sat back and watched the passing scenery. He was dressed for his role, his clothes a little flashier than necessary.

When the cab stopped in front of an apartment building, he glanced out the window and realized this must be her place.

"I'll be back in a few minutes," he said, then hopped out and went inside. He found her apartment easily enough. He tapped on the door and waited.

When the door opened, he stood there and stared. For a split second, he thought he had the wrong apartment.

The efficient-looking agent was gone. In her place was a woman who dressed to call attention to herself. There wasn't a red-blooded male around who wouldn't notice this woman.

She wore a scarlet leather skirt that barely covered her butt and a sheer white blouse that was held together by one button placed only a few inches above her waistline. He wouldn't have believed the woman to have as much cleavage as she now showed him . . . and the rest of the world.

High heels called attention to her shapely legs, while her new hairstyle and makeup erased all hint of the prim and proper woman he'd last seen in Ken's office. Her eyes now had a sultry look, and her mouth teased a man to sample its softness.

"I'll get my bag," she said after a rather lengthy pause, jolting Clint into the realization that he'd been standing there in her doorway staring at her as if he were some country yokel.

Clint cleared his throat and said, "They did a good job." He sounded hoarse. "I mean, you, uh, look sensational." His gaze kept returning to her legs, her cleavage and her face.

She paused in the act of reaching for her handbag. "Thanks," she replied dryly, grabbing her purse.

All right. So he shouldn't have sounded so shocked. Her transformation had startled him, that's all.

He tried to clarify his reaction. "Not that you don't always look— That is, you're a very attractive—"

"Cut the corn, Callaway. We don't have to go into our lovebird act until we land in Nevada." She stepped out into the hallway and closed the door, making certain it locked behind her.

She no longer sounded like agent Rousseau. Instead he suddenly realized— "My God, you *sound* like Sylvia. How'd the two of you get along, anyway?" He forced himself to maintain eye contact, absently noting the fact that it took forced concentration for him not to continue to mentally compile a list of her physical assets.

"Well, enough," she replied. "She's got quite a voice. It's a shame she never got the recognition to go with it." The elevator opened and they stepped inside. "My trunks are being shipped separately, I understand. What about yours?"

"My bag's in the taxi downstairs."

Clint caught himself becoming irritated when the cabbie practically fell all over himself opening the door for Gabrielle. She appeared totally unconcerned with the length of leg she exposed when she stepped into the taxi.

Had such an extreme dress style really been necessary for her to get into the new role she was playing?

Once inside the cab, he said in a voice meant only for her ears, "You're being billed as Gabrielle Grant. We decided your first name is exotic enough."

She glanced at him from the corner of her kohl-lined eye. "My mother will be touched by your endorsement, I'm sure."

She pulled out a compact and fussed with her hair, touched her nose with a powder puff and applied an even thicker coat of bright red lipstick to her already glowing mouth.

She had all the mannerisms down. Her voice had taken on a husky quality and she was suddenly using her eyes with devastating effect. Not even the cabbie had been immune to her slow appraisal of him. If Clint were honest, he'd admit—at least to himself—that her sultry look was having a definite effect on him, as well.

So much for believing that it was brains and charm a man first noticed in a woman.

"New threads?" she asked, touching the sleeve of his coat and lightly stroking his arm. He tensed at her touch before forcing himself to relax. He'd have to monitor his reactions to her, something he hadn't thought would be an issue on this operation.

He glanced down at the cheap plaid coat he'd been given to wear. "Yeah," he drawled. "Couldn't let you outclass me, now, could I, Angel-face?"

Her eyes sparkled with amusement but she kept any trace of a smile off her lips. Instead she stuck her lower lip out into a tiny pout. "I bet you never thought about getting me anything when you were out shopping, did you, Lover?"

He reached into his breast pocket and pulled out a long, narrow box. He handed it to her without a word.

She took it and opened it, letting out a squeal of delight. "Oh, Rocky! A diamond watch. Oh, you darling, darling man!"

Since the purpose of the watch was for her to be able to stay in touch with him at all times through the tiny transmitter inside, about which she'd already been briefed, he was unprepared for her enthusiastic response to what was only meant to be part of their surveillance equipment.

She launched herself into his arms, wrapping her arms around his neck and eagerly kissing him on the cheek, ear and mouth. "Aren't you just the sweetest thing? I swear, you must be able to read my mind."

Her perfume engulfed him in its heady scent and without a thought to possible consequences he wrapped his arms around her and kissed her back. His aim was much more precise than hers had been. He unerringly found her mouth.

The shock of her softness stunned him with a jolt of desire, catching him off guard. When she shyly opened her mouth, he immediately accepted what she was so generously offering.

The kiss hadn't been planned by either one of them. She had been practicing her role as his lover and he had gone along with it. The incendiary sparks weren't part of the role-playing and they both knew it.

Clint didn't care. Every muscle in his body had come to full alert, ready for action. He wasn't too sure that he would have been able to call a halt—although later he convinced himself that it was merely playacting and could have been stopped at any-time—if the taxi hadn't suddenly jolted to a halt. He jerked his mouth away from hers and held her tightly against his chest to prevent her from being thrown against the back seat, while he used his legs to brace them both.

Clint looked into the rearview mirror at the driver's red face. He'd obviously been paying more attention to what was going on in the back seat of his cab than to the heavy traffic surrounding them. Consequently, the cab had almost rear-ended the car in front of them.

"How about watching the road, buddy?" he growled, using the interruption as an excuse to disentangle himself from Gabrielle.

She'd caught him off guard and unprepared, and it irritated him. He wasn't used to working with a partner, that's all. He'd just have to remember to keep his guard up at all times.

Gabrielle looked as shaken as he felt, which gave him some comfort. But not much.

"You almost caused us to have a wreck, Angel-face," he growled, patting her thigh. Only after his hand cupped the warm, muscled, nylon-clad leg did he decide that from now on he'd better keep his hands to himself if he didn't want further distractions. "Save all that enthusiasm for later, okay?"

She gave him a saucy grin. "And you'd better wipe off some of that lipstick, Lover. It's really not your shade."

Clint reached into his back pocket and fished out a clean handkerchief, wiping it across his mouth. It came away with smears of bright red. "Thanks a lot," he muttered, half under his breath.

She batted her long, artificial lashes. "Anytime, Sugar. Anyplace. You know how I feel about you."

Clint was relieved to see that they were approaching the airport. He couldn't help wondering why Gabrielle Rousseau was wasting her talents working for the government. With her acting skills, she should be auditioning in Hollywood.

What bothered him was his reaction to her kiss. She had not made the gesture personal; he had done that. He couldn't understand why he'd had the sudden urge to make the kiss a real one.

Now he was sorry that he had because it put their assignment on a new level. Playing her protector was one thing. The reality was that Gabrielle Rousseau could look after herself. She had one of the finest marksman ratings in the department and her self-defense scores were high.

"We're here, Rocky, honey," she announced, nudging him with her elbow.

"Rocky?" he muttered as the driver got out of the car and opened the trunk to get Clint's bag.

She winked at him. "It goes with the suit, ya know what I mean?"

He just shook his head and got out of the cab. After helping her out and being given another fine display of long, well-shaped legs, he paid the cab-driver and picked up his bag.

Gabrielle kept up her nonstop chatter all the way through the airport, while they waited in line to board, and once they found their seats. She sat by the window, he the aisle.

"All right, already," he finally said. "Enough, enough. I'm impressed with your homework, your looks and your act but save a little of it for when we get there, okay?"

She grinned before reaching for her compact once again for a quick peek. In a low voice, she said,

"Sorry, guess I got a little carried away. I've never had an assignment like this before."

"You could have fooled me. I thought you had show business in your blood from the performance you've been giving."

"What about your performance, cowboy?"

"Mine?" He glanced at the clothes he wore. "What are you talking about?"

"The kiss that almost caused our cabbie to wreck the car." Her cheeks appeared rosier, although it could be from all the makeup she was wearing. "Wasn't that a little much?"

He had the grace to nod. "Sorry. I was out of line," he grudgingly admitted. He couldn't resist adding, "Guess I'm not used to women throwing themselves at me like that."

"Really?" She glanced out the window as she said, "That's not what I've heard."

"What are you talking about?"

She turned her head slowly as though reluctant to continue their conversation. "Nothing."

"Are you saying I'm supposed to be some kind of playboy type?"

"Let's just say that some of the women working in the department seem to find speculations regarding your personal life more exciting than talking about your role as an agent."

"That's ridiculous."

She chuckled. "Of course it is. Who could possibly be interested in a man with your looks, who's a member of a wealthy, famous family, a man whose reputation in the field has become legendary—not to mention mysterious and sinister. Turns me off at the mere thought of getting involved with someone like that." She reached for the airline magazine and began to thumb through it.

He knew he should dismiss the conversation from his mind. She was baiting him, that's all. But then again, maybe there was a message in there that he'd missed.

"Is that supposed to be amusing?"

"Not at all. I find it rather sad, actually."

Now what was she talking about? "Oh?" he asked, adjusting his seat. "How do you figure that?"

She looked over at him with a half smile on her face. "You poor dear, you really have it rough. You can never know if a woman is attracted to you, the man, or to the aura of power and control that surrounds you. Must be really tough on your ego."

Clint stiffened. Was she deliberately trying to be insulting? "My ego is just fine, thank you very much," he replied in a level tone.

She patted his hand. "Good for you. Now, if you don't mind, I'm going to catch up on my sleep. These past few days have been really hectic."

If there was a way for him to contact Ken at that moment, he would tell him in no uncertain terms why he preferred working alone. *Who in the hell does this woman think she is?*

Being born into the Callaway clan wasn't anything over which he'd had control, for God's sake. As a child growing up in Texas, Clint had been too young to understand how well-known his father, Cole, and his two uncles, Cameron and Cody, were in the state.

Even his older brother, Tony, had made a name for himself in the rodeo world, but their dad was the one who ran the business empire known as Callaway Enterprises.

He had to give his dad credit for not trying to pressure him into following in his footsteps. By the time he was in high school, Clint knew he wanted to work in the intelligence community. Once he'd received the offer his senior year at the eastern university he'd attended, he'd never looked back.

The one thing he'd never done was make a career out of chasing women! For the most part, he hadn't had time to devote to a relationship and he'd never cared for casual flings. He was competitive enough to want to be the best at whatever career he chose, which meant that all his energies went toward improving his professional skills.

Now he was beginning to wonder if he'd been too focused on his career. He wasn't at all certain he knew how to handle this new aspect of Gabrielle's character. He knew this was just an assignment, but he'd never been placed in such a provocative situation before.

The only other time he'd worked with a woman was several years ago when a child had been involved and the agency had thought a woman would be better able to calm a child's fears. His assigned partner had been in her late forties, a motherly type who'd done her job well.

He certainly wasn't familiar with the glitter of Las Vegas nor the scantily dressed women who made their living there, but he was fully prepared to deal with the matter as a professional, partner or no partner.

He settled back in his chair and closed his eyes, mentally counting the days until they would have this particular operation successfully completed so that he would be on his own once again.

Chapter 3

Gabrielle awoke when the intercom of the plane came on and the captain announced they were now making their descent into Las Vegas. She raised her seat-back to its upright position and peered out the window.

Las Vegas looked like a dusty mirage scattered across a desert surrounded by barren mountains. Bright green squares of lawns gave credence to the notion that there was water underground, waiting to be tapped.

Maybe that was the way she could view this assignment. Her life, although not strictly arid or dry, had stayed within certain bounds since she'd begun working for the government. Now she had an opportunity to blossom, as it were, by strutting her stuff on stage and employing the singing techniques she'd learned when she was in school. That is, of course, as long as she could count on Howard to know in which key each song had to be played in order for her to be able to hit all the notes.

She found herself humming the tune to "If They Could See Me Now," from the Broadway play, *Sweet Charity.*

"Do you always wake up in such a good mood?" Clint growled near her ear.

She straightened and looked around at him. "Your technique could use some work, Lover-boy. Or is that frown permanently etched on your forehead?" She wasn't certain why she was enjoying needling him so. Perhaps it was because he'd made it so obvious that he didn't want to work with her and now he was stuck with her.

He was one cool customer. Other than a slight tightening of his jaw and narrowing of his eyes, he showed no reaction to her jibe. Of course the frown didn't disappear, either.

She waited for his response, realizing that she was enjoying herself immensely in her new role. It was as if she'd shed the persona that had served her so well all these years. Now she could be as zany as she wished with no one to call her on her behavior. She was an entertainer, after all.

The plane touched down and rolled to the end of the runway before turning and moving toward the gate.

"At least we don't have to stop at the luggage claim," Clint said, reaching into the overhead bin for his bag. "Come on, let's get out of here."

Ever the gentleman, she decided with a grin. He did step into the aisle and allow her to go ahead of him, which was a good thing. Her first steps reminded her that she was now wearing ridiculously high heels and would have to learn to move with a mincing step or she'd fall flat on her face.

Once inside the terminal, she clung to Clint's arm for support, while he did his best to ignore her inane chatter. Actually she was having trouble coming up with things to say and felt some relief once they found a taxi and were on their way to the casino hotel.

Clint had been his usual taciturn self since they landed. She figured he must be a throwback to some ancestor who rode the range and spoke only to his horse and herd of cattle.

"What's the smile for?" he asked as their driver turned the cab into the imposing entrance of their hotel.

"Was I smiling?" she absently replied, peering through the window of the cab. "This place is huge, isn't it?"

"I suppose," he replied, frowning. After a moment, he asked, "When's your first rehearsal?"

She quickly peeked into her purse and checked her schedule. "This afternoon at three, why?"

"I thought we'd grab some lunch, then look around before you have to report to the production people."

"Sounds good to me. It never hurts to get a lay of the land."

Once inside, Gabrielle's eyes widened when she saw the huge area devoted entirely to gambling. The slot machines were arranged in long lines like soldiers standing at attention. She waited at the reservation desk with Clint and looked around, amazed at the number of people gambling at this time of day.

"Ah, yes, we have your reservations right here, Ms. Grant," he said with a brilliant smile. He did a rapid survey of her outfit without missing a beat. "Welcome to our fair city."

She gave Clint a quick glance before giving the clerk her most seductive smile. "I'm just thrilled to death to be here. Most of my work has been done overseas, you know." She flicked her eyelashes before asking the question that was vital to their operation. "Did my trunks arrive all right? The airlines can be so careless at times."

Eager to give her the news, the clerk said, "Oh, yes. They were delivered earlier this morning. We had them placed in your room for you. I think you'll find everything satisfactory."

She frowned, giving another quick glance at Clint. "Room?" she repeated stiffly. "I was told that I would be given a suite."

"Oh, yes, of course. I didn't make myself clear. I should have said your bedroom."

"Ahh, that's fine, then." She fluttered her lashes and rewarded him with another provocative smile. "Thank you for all your help."

Clint watched her performance without expression, taking the plastic card that served as a key from her, then lightly holding on to her elbow while they walked the several acres between the reservation desk and the elevator.

They rode the elevator in silence. Clint politely helped her off the elevator when they reached their floor, adroitly preventing her from falling when the stiletto-thin heel of one of her shoes caught in the crack between the elevator and the floor.

"Thanks," she murmured, but he didn't reply.

Once they spotted the room number Clint opened the door and waved her inside. As soon as she walked in, she gave a quick sigh of relief to see a spacious living area luxuriously decorated. Open doors at opposite ends of the room revealed the location of their bedrooms.

"Afraid you were going to have to share a room with me?" Clint asked, moving around the room and making a cursory inspection.

She gave him a quick glance before walking over to a table that held an elegant arrangement of flowers. "I'd do whatever was necessary, of course." She tossed the words over her shoulder. "However, I would be more comfortable with a room of my own."

She turned and with as much dignity as possible considering her attire walked into one of the bedrooms. It was a great exit line. Unfortunately the room showed no sign of her things and she was forced to walk back into the area where Clint stood, his hands in his pockets, looking out the window.

"The trunks should be in the other bedroom," she said, and they both went to unpack them. Much of the equipment they needed that would have caused questions on the plane were in those trunks.

In addition to her costumes was the equipment they would need to conduct their surveillance.

"You're going to be seen out in public in this?" Clint asked, holding up a thin piece of material decorated with sparkles and feathers.

"That's the general idea."

"Unbelievable." He stared at the garment with stern disapproval.

"You're sounding like a father, you know."

He ignored her. Checking his watch, he said, "We've got a couple of hours before you need to rehearse. Let's see how much ground we can cover in that amount of time." He was all brisk competence, making sure the door was locked, checking the hallway for emergency exits, then punching the button for the elevator.

Once downstairs, Gabrielle was amused to notice the second glances Clint got from various women as the two of them checked out the casino. So much for attempting to blend in with the clientele of the casino. Then again, maybe he just looked the part of a man who enjoyed women, causing them to unconsciously respond.

She had to agree. Clint was quite a man. She didn't have to do much pretending to convince people she felt safer in his company.

Clint sat at the back of the room and watched the performers as well as those who had come to be entertained. They had been in Vegas for two days now, rehearsing and getting to know their surroundings.

During that time Clint had been keeping an eye on their quarry—studying his routine, his habits and his act. The illusionist was good at what he did. Clint could see the ego of Raphael Romero onstage. No doubt he enjoyed outwitting the law enforcement people on two continents. Clint knew they had a tough adversary here. However, there was no doubt in his mind that they'd get him.

Gabrielle was on next. It was past midnight, local time, and this would be her third performance that day. She had to be exhausted.

She'd been busy with her rehearsals since they'd arrived, spending a great deal of time backstage getting to know the other members of the revue.

One stroke of luck was that the women shared a dressing room. She had returned to their suite each day with stories she'd picked up from the other entertainers.

Ken had been right about that, at least.

Romero had two female assistants. Gabrielle had reported that they didn't join in with the others much, although she was making it a point to become friendly with them. The plan was to plant listening devices in some of the equipment and personal belongings in hopes of picking up unguarded conversations.

So far, so good. Their plans were still on schedule.

The curtains lifted to the sound of a piano softly playing the blues. A blue-white spotlight shone down on the woman standing in the curve of that piano. Damn, but she looked good up there, as though she'd been born to play the part.

Gabrielle held the microphone in her hand as though cuddling a lover's hand. Her dress glittered with sparkles that seemed to dance around her body. The thin material clung to her curves, enhancing the illusion that her body was barely veiled.

Every time he heard her husky contralto voice, Clint felt his body respond, as though the sound activated all sorts of switches inside him. He had a hunch every man in the room was affected in the same way. She used a subtle technique where she appeared to be singing directly to each male in the audience, making it seem that her most soulful wish was to be with him. Alone.

Clint glanced around at the audience and was surprised to find the women just as caught up in Gabrielle's words.

Sylvia had certainly taught her technique and style but it was Gabrielle and her voice who were mesmerizing the audience.

By the time she finished, the room was awash in applause, just as it had been for the other performances. If she was looking for a second career, she'd certainly found one!

Clint left his table while she was still taking her bows. It was time for his performance to begin. He walked backstage and was waiting when Gabrielle stepped into the wings.

"Not bad, Angel-face. Not bad at all," he said, pulling her to him and nuzzling her neck. "I'm really proud of you," he added, sincerely.

She threw her arms around him. "Oh, Rocky, you're so sweet." She exuberantly kissed him, skillfully missing his mouth. Then she grabbed his hand and tugged. "C'mon back, and I'll introduce you to the others now that we're done for the night."

Romero's assistants were just coming out of the dressing room. They were now in street clothes, with no makeup and their wigs removed. He wouldn't have recognized them as being the same women he'd seen earlier onstage.

Gabrielle introduced him to everyone, clinging to his arm possessively while she chattered on about who did what onstage and off. Clint leaned against the doorjamb and gave them his most cynical, world-weary smile.

Eventually Romero stepped out of another dressing room, a towel thrown around his neck. He was about five-ten, maybe a hundred and fifty pounds, very sleek, very Latin, very aware of his good looks.

"Gabrielle," he said, holding out his hand and looking at her with soulful eyes. "You were magnificent tonight. We must talk, *chiquita*. I could help you a great deal in your career."

Clint slowly straightened. "What makes you think she needs help?" he asked with menace. "She's been doing just fine without any assistance from anyone else."

Gabrielle tugged at Clint's hand again, this time pulling him over to where Romero stood. "Rafe, I want you to meet Rocky. He's my manager," she said in such a way that there was absolutely no doubt in anyone's mind that he was much more than her manager.

"I see," Romero replied, looking Clint up and down with disdain. He returned his attention to Gabrielle. "I could make you a star," he said in a low voice, not meant for anyone else's ears. Clint had trouble keeping a straight face. He wondered how anyone thought that sort of line would still work.

Gabrielle glowed. "Really? How?"

Romero flickered a glance to Clint before replying. "Why don't we discuss it over dinner?"

Clint slipped his arm possessively around Gabrielle's shoulders. "I don't think so," he said with a smile that gave no hint of amusement. "Gabrielle's had a long week. Besides, she needs her rest. Maybe some other time."

The two men stared at each other in silence.

"I *am* hungry, Rocky honey," Gabrielle said hopefully.

"Then I'll see that you get fed," Clint said. "C'mon. Let's get out of here."

"I've gotta change, honey, but I'll hurry." She smiled at Romero. "I'll see you tomorrow, Rafe. Maybe we can talk then," she said, then hurried to her dressing room.

Clint folded his arms and leaned against the closed door. "Whatever you think you're planning," he said in a low voice to Romero, "you can forget it. Nobody barges in on my territory. Nobody."

"I think you forget who you're talking to," Romero said softly, idly stroking the handle of the knife he wore at his waist as part of his act.

Clint lifted an eyebrow. "So why don't you tell me?" he sneered.

Romero looked him up and down as though dismissing him. "I have connections. I could get the right people in here to see her. I could—"

"Yeah, I'm real impressed with your talents, amigo, both on and off the stage. But you're going to have to practice them on somebody else. She's already taken."

Clint was enjoying the hell out of his role of swaggering male, claiming his property. It was obvious that it didn't take much to tap into a male's caveman instincts. In fact, it was downright comfortable to be making threatening sounds to other males. He almost laughed out loud at the thought.

Romero turned on his heel and went back into his dressing room, slamming the door.

When Gabrielle came out of the dressing room, she'd removed the stage makeup, but still looked flashy in a sparkly dress that stopped midthigh.

"I'm ready, Rocky," she said seductively, leaning into him and rubbing her breasts across his chest.

He dropped his arm across her shoulders and held her against him. "So am I, baby, so am I."

Clint wasn't too certain how much of that particular sentiment was part of the act.

"I expected to see the two of you pawing the ground and shaking your antlers any minute there," Gabrielle said to him once they returned to their suite. She paused when she saw a table set up for a meal, a warming cart nearby. "Oh! You ordered dinner."

"Yeah. I thought you'd like a chance to relax for a few hours," he said over his shoulder, making certain the door was secured for the night.

She sighed. "I'm more than ready, I assure you. If you don't mind waiting for just a minute, I think I'll change into something a little more comfortable."

"Go ahead. I'll get the food out."

Gabrielle had no sooner gone into her bedroom than there was a knock at the door to the suite.

Clint peered through the peephole and saw a woman wearing a hotel uniform. "Who is it?" he asked impatiently.

"Room service, sir."

"We haven't eaten yet. I'll ring when—"

She held up a bottle. "This was left off the cart."

He stepped back and unlocked the door. The woman standing there was blond and petite. "I don't remember ordering anything but coffee and water to drink."

She smiled, looking positively angelic. "Compliments of the management, sir. We wanted to make your stay as pleasant as possible." She offered him the expensive-looking bottle.

He shrugged and took it, then reached into his pocket for a tip. She immediately shook her head and stepped back. "Oh, no. But thank you."

"What's your name?" he asked, feeling as though he knew her, even though he could swear he'd never laid eyes on her before.

"Aurora."

"Oh. Well, thank you, Aurora." He held up the bottle and smiled.

"Enjoy it," she said shyly.

As soon as the door closed, Aurora chuckled. If only he knew what this particular elixir had in store for them. It was a combination truth serum and hallucinogen. For the next few hours these two independent, stubborn people were going to believe that they were in Las Vegas on their honeymoon.

By morning, of course, they would remember nothing of what happened, at least not consciously. But on a deeper, soul-level, these two would know of the bond that had been formed.

It was going to be interesting to see how they would react to each other.

With a beatific smile, Aurora slipped away.

Clint closed the door thoughtfully, relocking it, then found a pair of long-stemmed glasses. He opened the bottle and was filling two glasses when Gabrielle came out of her room. She wore a fuzzy robe with matching house slippers.

"I managed to smuggle a few of my own things into the clothes to use in the privacy of the suite," she said by way of explanation.

At least she was decently covered for a change. Without makeup and with her hair pulled back from her face, she looked more like the woman he knew.

"What are you celebrating?" she asked, nodding toward the bottle and glasses.

"Compliments of the management. Thought I'd open it so we could enjoy it with dinner."

"I'm starved. All that nervous energy burns up the calories." They removed the covered dishes from the warming tray and placed them on the table.

He seated her and handed her one of the glasses, toasting her with the other. "You're doing a great job, you know. You even have me convinced that you were a European singing sensation."

She grinned. "Thank God for Sylvia. I couldn't have done it without her." They drank from their glasses. "Mmm. This is scrumptious. What is it?"

"I'm not sure. I've never heard of the label before. We can always pretend it's ambrosia of the gods, right?"

She laughed and took another sip before attacking her meal.

There was very little conversation during dinner. At one point Clint felt a little strange. Not quite dizzy... at least, not exactly. More disoriented. He tried to focus on Gabrielle's face and became absorbed in studying each and every feature...how her lashes, not the fake ones but her own dark ones, veiled her eyes. She looked at him inquiringly. He'd never before noticed the tiny smattering of freckles across the bridge of her patrician nose, or the way her eyes danced when she was amused, such as now.

"Do I have a smudge on my nose," she asked with a grin, "or food on my face?"

He found her smile enchanting—the way the corners turned up slightly on either side, the soft fullness of her lower lip. He badly wanted to taste and touch her mouth again, this time without all the stuff on her face.

"Clint?"

Her voice sounded husky and he had a sudden thought of what she must sound like first thing in the morning, after a night of intense loving...with him.

"Would you like more wine?" he asked, picking up the bottle. Without waiting for an answer, he filled their glasses once again. "To us," he said, toasting her and touching the rim of his glass to hers.

Her eyes widened slightly, then she gave an embarrassed laugh. "Is there an us, Clint?"

"I certainly hope so," he said. "Why else would we be here on our honeymoon?"

She blinked, then absently glanced down at the sparkling ring on her finger, which matched the one on his finger. She touched her temple as though slightly dazed. "That drink must be potent stuff. For a while there I seemed to have forgotten we were married."

He smiled. "I'm having trouble believing it myself." He glanced at her plate. "Are you through eating?"

"I guess," she murmured.

"I thought we could sit out on the balcony for a while and enjoy the night view." He took her hand and slowly pulled her from her chair, right into his arms. He settled his mouth over hers with a sigh.

Oh, yes. She tasted as good as she looked, and she looked fabulous to him. She relaxed against him, returning his kiss with unfeigned enthusiasm.

He cautioned himself to go slow. Reluctantly he drew away from her and led her out onto the balcony. He sat down on the chaise longue and drew her against him so that her back rested against his chest and she was nestled between his thighs.

"I'll never forget the first time I saw you," he mused.

She glanced up at him. "Tell me."

"I'd just gotten back from an assignment in Paris. I noticed you as soon as I walked into the office."

She chuckled. "Sure you did."

He ignored her comment. "You were wearing a dark suit that fit snugly around your waist and I had a sudden urge to wrap my hands around you . . . like this—" he placed his hands on either side of her waist "—to see if you were as tiny as you looked. I'd just gotten to the point where I was checking out your legs when you turned around and caught me."

"At which time you met my eyes and refused to look anywhere else."

"Absolutely. Can't afford to be accused of treating a fellow agent with anything less than full respect."

"I remember that day. One of the first things I remember about you is that you never smiled . . . and your eyes were like black steel. I pitied any suspect having to face you and attempting to lie."

"Who would have believed that we would end up like this?"

"Yes. I distinctly remember hearing the rumor that you were a loner who never got deeply involved with anyone . . . and absolutely no one with whom you worked."

"That's true enough."

"So what happened?"

That same sense of disorientation swept over him. "I'm not certain. I suppose I got tired of fighting my feelings where you were concerned. How about you?"

"It's really difficult to explain." She didn't speak right away and when she did, her words startled him. "You see, I never intended to get married."

"Never?"

"No. I watched my mother grow old before her time trying to take care of me and my younger brothers and sisters. My dad did as little as possible at home. He worked in a steel mill on swing shift. When he was home, he sat in front of the television until it was time to eat or go to bed. It was my mother's job to keep up with the house and all us kids. Growing up, most of my time after school was spent looking after the little ones."

"How many were there?"

"Six. I was almost five before my brother was born. Then she seemed to have a baby every year after that."

"That must have been tough."

"I just knew that I didn't want a life like that. I worked hard to make the grades necessary to get a scholarship to go away to school. My freedom is more important to me than anything else."

"And yet you married me."

She was quiet for a long time and Clint had to consciously resist holding her even closer to him. He didn't want her to slip away from him, even mentally or emotionally.

"It does seem rather sudden, doesn't it?" she finally said, sounding puzzled.

"Yeah. But I guess being in Vegas made the idea feasible."

"What is your family going to think?"

That certainly gave him food for thought. "Well, I guess my folks will be pleased I'm finally making a commitment to someone. Of course Cade will give me a bad time, since he's always insisted I'd marry before he does. I disagreed with him vehemently on more than one occasion, as I recall."

"Cade's your brother?"

"Uh-huh."

"He's older?"

"Nope. I arrived twenty minutes before he did."

She sat up and turned to look at him. "You have a twin brother?"

"Isn't that what I just said?"

"I can't believe this. You never told me that. Are you identical twins?"

"Yes. Of course the family can tell us apart, but when we were in school together, we were often mistaken for each other."

"What was it like, having a twin?"

"I have no way to compare it with anything else. I guess I just accepted it."

"Did you have a lot in common?"

"We both loved sports. Especially football. I played quarterback, while he was a receiver. Coach said it was uncanny how I could always find him on the field, no matter how well covered either of us was. We're both competitive, but I think that's a family trait. I was always considered by everyone as the quiet one, while Cade has always been a charming flirt.''

She touched his face with her finger, tracing a line along his jaw. ''Nobody could accuse you of being a flirt, that's for sure.'' She studied his face, bewildered by their situation. ''I still can't believe we're married. It's so sudden.''

''Makes sense to me. No doubt it was the only way the two of us would consider such a thing. I'm pleased we just did it without making a fuss.''

''You mean notifying family and making plans for a wedding?''

''Yeah, although knowing my folks, they'll insist on throwing us a big party to celebrate.''

''I'm looking forward to meeting your family... and your flirtatious brother.'' She settled back against his shoulder and kissed him—a lazy, lingering kiss that, nevertheless, had his heart racing. By the time he was able to draw some air into his lungs, Clint knew he wasn't going to be able to hang on to his control much longer.

He wanted Gabrielle in a way he'd never wanted a woman before. He felt as though he would die if he didn't make love to her soon.

She was his wife now, wasn't she? What was he waiting for? With that thought, he stood and pulled her into his arms. Then he picked her up, carrying her into his bedroom.

The sheets were already pulled back invitingly. He leaned down and carefully placed her on the bed. Suddenly self-conscious, he hastily pulled off his clothes, then stretched out beside her.

Chapter 4

Gabrielle hastily removed her shoes and untied her robe as soon as Clint placed her on the bed. She wore a plain cotton gown underneath. Oh, how she wished she had something more glamorous to wear for Clint. She wanted to be alluring, to make him want her so badly that—

She caught her breath at the sight of Clint peeling off his clothes. He'd removed his shirt and for the first time in her life she was watching a man undress. His chest was broad and muscular, a thick thatch of black hair covering the expanse, then arrowing downward toward his belly button and beyond.

He unfastened his belt and drew off his pants. She no longer concerned herself about being appealing to him. There was no doubt that he wanted her. By the time the last garment was removed, he was stretched out beside her, playing with the lace around the scooped neck of her gown.

"I feel as though I'm at a distinct disadvantage here," he whispered. "You have on more clothes than I do." He tugged on the gown until she shifted and allowed him to pull it off of her. "Ah, that's so much better."

She shivered at the look in his eyes. When he cupped her breast with his hand she caught her breath, almost afraid to breathe.

"Relax, I'm not going to do anything to hurt you. You must know that."

"I, uh, yes, I know you wouldn't. It's just that— I mean, I'm not used to having someone look at me like that."

"Like what?" he asked, sounding amused.

"Like a starving man at a banquet, not sure where he wants to begin."

Clint laughed. "That's exactly how I feel, except for one thing." He leaned over and gave her a long, thorough kiss, before saying, "I know *exactly* where I want to begin." He placed his mouth at the crest of her breast and gently flicked the rosy peak with his tongue, causing it to harden.

Gabrielle shifted restlessly, feeling a tightening sensation forming deep within her. She could feel her heart racing and hear her own uneven breathing. No one had ever touched her so intimately before. She stroked his shoulder, feeling the muscled warmth beneath her fingertips.

This was Clint, the man she loved. This was—

Loved? How could she love him? She didn't even know him...and yet, they were married. Why would—

He shifted, trailing a row of kisses down between her breasts, along her stomach and abdomen, his feathery touch causing her to quiver in reaction.

She lost her train of thought.

Instead she gave herself up to his expert lovemaking.

By the time he moved over her, she was whimpering with need. She clung to him, not certain what else to do. There was something she wanted from him, but she wasn't sure what until he slowly joined them together.

Instinctively she moved her legs so that they were gripping him tightly. He kissed her, his breathing as uneven as her own.

"Oh, honey, you're so tight. I didn't— I'm sorry, I meant to wait longer, but— I—"

"It's all right. I had no idea it would feel so good. I mean—"

His chuckle sounded a little breathless. "I know exactly what you mean. I feel as though I've never made love with anyone before tonight."

"Me, too," she admitted, because it was the truth.

He picked up the pace. She could feel something inside of her growing tighter and tighter until suddenly she seemed to explode inside. Her groan matched his as he gave one final lunge and gathered her into a fierce grip as their two bodies fused into one.

Gabrielle wondered if this was what dying felt like, this lightness of spirit, this wonderful sense of rightness and serenity. Nothing else mattered but this feeling of contentment as she clung to this man who had shown her the beauty of physical union.

He shifted his body and she let out a little squeak of protest.

"I'm too heavy for you, love," he whispered, rolling to his side without letting her go.

She had to admit that she could breathe easier with the shift in their positions.

"Did I hurt you?" he asked.

"Oh, no. You were wonderful."

Although he was still breathing hard, he managed to chuckle. "Hardly that. I don't seem to have much control when I'm around you."

"I'm glad. You always seem to be in complete control of yourself. That's one of the first things I noticed about you . . . that, and your aloofness."

Since they were lying chest to breast at the time, he just smiled. "I'm not very aloof at the moment."

"I know. I can't seem to remember when you began to change toward me."

"Me either, but I'm glad I did."

She placed a soft kiss on his mouth. "This has been a very special night."

"Mmm," he said, more than half asleep. "We'll have many more of them, just like this one," he murmured before breathing deeply and drifting into sleep.

Gabrielle sighed with deep contentment and joined him in a dreamless sleep.

Aurora stood at the end of the bed, watching the sleeping couple. Yes, she had played a trick on them, but she'd felt it was necessary . . . for two more stubborn people she'd never met.

Clint refused to consider making a commitment to anyone, while Gabrielle was afraid she would relive her mother's life. Both would find out soon enough that they were wrong in what they thought a relationship could be.

She hoped she had given them a taste of what the future held for them, if only they would allow themselves to believe in the transforming power of love.

A great deal would depend on how they accepted what had happened between them. There was no going back from the steps they had taken tonight.

* * *

Gabrielle stirred from her deep sleep, feeling unusually pleased with herself. Without opening her eyes she stretched luxuriously, only to freeze when her foot brushed against a warm leg.

Her eyes flew open and she sat up, staring in horror at the other side of the bed. Was she still asleep and dreaming or was she actually in bed with fellow agent, Clint Callaway?

He lay sprawled on his stomach with his head half-buried beneath a pillow, but there was no mistaking who he was. His broad shoulders were uncovered. In fact, the sheet barely covered his bare bottom.

Only then did she realize that she was just as bare as he.

Gabrielle sprang from the bed, frantically fumbling for her gown and robe, then dashed out the door, through the living area and into the bedroom she'd taken as hers.

She closed and locked the door, then fell against it as though all the hounds of hell were pursuing her.

What in the world had she done? Last night was just a fuzzy blur to her. She remembered changing into her robe in order to have dinner.

They'd eaten. Or had they? They must have eaten.

Had she drunk anything? No, of course not. She never drank. There had been iced tea and coffee, but no alcoholic beverages.

So how had it happened that she'd awakened in her assigned partner's bed wearing not a stitch of clothing? She could feel her entire body heat with embarrassment. Was he aware that she'd been in his bed? If so, what must he think of her? She'd always prided herself on being professional, leaving the difference in gender out of the working relationship she had with her fellow agents.

Gabrielle wandered into her bathroom, dropping the clothing she'd been clutching in front of her, and stared at her image in the mirror.

Outside of the blond streaks in her hair she looked just as she'd always looked—a little too slender, not overly endowed. In short, nothing to lure a man into unbridled lust.

How silly to think that something might have actually happened between them. Wouldn't she remember if they had actually...well...been intimate? And yet...there was nothing innocent about waking up to find herself in bed with a man, both of them nude. Why else would she have taken off her gown if it wasn't for—?

No! She couldn't have. She wouldn't have.

The whole thing was preposterous, she decided, taking a rational approach to the problem. She'd been unusually tired, having been up for almost twenty-four hours. Somehow, someway, she must have gotten up to go to the bathroom during the night and wandered into the wrong bedroom. She refused to contemplate any possible reasons for removing her gown.

Well, at least she could be thankful for small blessings. Clint had still been asleep when she woke up. How could she have possibly explained her presence in his bed if he'd awakened first?

She cringed at the thought.

Gabrielle turned on the shower and stepped inside, allowing the steaming water to soothe her. At least she'd learned one thing. From now on she would lock her door before going to bed at night. Only she would know that it wasn't locked in order to keep her partner out, but to discourage any sleepwalking activities with which she seemed to be suddenly afflicted.

Clint's wristwatch alarm started beeping repeatedly in his ear and he groaned in regret. He stirred only enough to shut it off, feeling entirely too engrossed in his dream to give up and face the day.

And what a dream it was. He rolled over onto his back and pulled his pillow to his chest with a smile of contentment. Gabrielle had been so loving and receptive to his lovemaking. He hadn't wanted to let her go. Gabrielle had—

Clint came wide-awake at the thought of Agent Rousseau. He sat up in bed and rapidly shook his head. Was he crazy? Dreaming about Gabrielle as though they had been—

What was the matter with him, anyway? He must have been more tired than he thought when he finally got to bed last night.

He shoved his hand through his hair, causing it to stand up in spikes. What he needed was a shower—a very cold shower—and a strong cup of hot coffee. Otherwise he'd never be able to face her again.

By the time Clint showered, shaved and dressed, he realized he hadn't heard Gabrielle stirring at all. Of course he hadn't really expected to, not with the spacious room that separated them.

He picked up the phone to call for breakfast, then decided to wait to see what she wanted to eat. Instead he called the surveillance boys who were monitoring the bugs Gabrielle had planted.

After calling a special number that scrambled the call before forwarding it, he finally got in touch with the team.

"Any luck?"

"Depends on what we wanted to know" came the drawled response. "This guy seems to believe his own press about being a Latin lover extraordinaire."

"Other than that."

"Maybe. He made a couple of calls that were obviously in code. He's supposed to be meeting with someone before the afternoon rehearsals."

"Somebody watching him?"

"But of course, oh fearless leader. Never worry, we're on the job. How did Gabrielle do yesterday?"

"Quite well. It's hard to believe she got her training singing in college and in a church choir. She had the men in the audience howling for more."

"Good for her."

"I'll stay in touch. If there are any sudden changes, you can leave a message for me, Uncle Charlie."

The other agent laughed. "Yeah, I'll do that... Rocky."

Clint hung up the phone just as Gabrielle's door opened. He glanced around and was unprepared for the jolt he felt when he saw her standing in the doorway watching him.

Must be the clothes, he told himself. He still hadn't gotten used to the amount of leg exposed by those short skirts she was wearing. He had an almost uncontrollable desire to walk across the room and kiss her good-morning.

He must really be getting into the role of Rocky.

"I was going to order some coffee and breakfast. Anything special you want?" he asked, reaching for the phone.

She cleared her throat. "Toast and coffee would be fine." She waited for him to call in their order before she nervously touched the low neckline of her top. "Isn't this a little much?" she asked. He could see that she was embarrassed by the cleavage exposed.

"For the agent, maybe so, but for the performer, it looks right in character."

She shrugged and smiled. "Guess it takes me a while to get into the role first thing in the day."

"When do you have to be at rehearsals today?"

"I'm scheduled at four, why?"

"I don't know. I thought we might visit the casino for a while, blend in with the tourists, lose a little money, that sort of thing."

"Good idea. Have you talked to the crew?"

"Yeah. The signals are coming in loud and clear, it seems. It's just a matter of waiting to see what we can get."

Her grin was filled with mischief. "I hid one of the bugs in the lining of a bra."

"That would certainly explain some of the conversations we picked up."

She wandered over to one of the windows and looked out. "Do you have any idea how long I'm expected to perform here?"

"I think we booked you for the week. It would look suspicious if you left before then."

She turned away and faced him, wrapping her arms around her waist in a protective gesture. "Do you think Raphael is going to pursue this thing with me?"

"Oh, yes. There's no doubt in my mind that the man intends to make another conquest."

She shivered. "Please. Not on an empty stomach."

He grinned. "You mean you don't find him irresistibly fascinating?"

"I've never met any man I found irresistibly fascinating," she said firmly. Her cheeks suddenly glowed and she turned away from him once again. "Oh, we have a balcony. I hadn't noticed." Without looking around, she slid the glass door open and stepped outside.

She appeared a little nervous to him this morning. More vulnerable, somehow, than she'd seemed to be when they first arrived. Strange, but he found the trait endearing. He'd always found her to be relaxed with the men with whom she worked, and yesterday she had played the role of enchanting entertainer with saucy aplomb.

This morning she appeared to be more human, somehow. He wanted to reassure her that everything would work out all right, although he had no idea why he felt such a strong urge to do so. After all, they were both doing a job they were assigned to do.

He wasn't certain why he was engulfed in these feelings. Maybe he was just getting into the role.

A sudden flashback to his dream of the night before caused him to pause, his heart racing. Whew! He was certainly getting into the role of lover...at least in his dreams.

Chapter 5

Gabrielle finished with her rehearsal and headed to her dressing room. She felt really wiped out, for some reason. And her body seemed to be unusually tender in certain intimate areas, which she found puzzling. She could find no explanation for the tenderness in her breasts and the slight ache lower.

What was worse was how she was reacting whenever she was in Clint's presence. At least he wasn't aware that sometime during the night she must have crawled into his bed, but she felt ill at ease around him now. It must have something to do with seeing him bare and asleep. She knew she wouldn't have been able to handle his seeing her in a similar situation.

Plus she couldn't seem to put thoughts of him out of her mind. She kept having this strong urge to touch him, as though she wanted nothing more than to run her fingers through his hair or to caress his face.

She must need a vacation. As soon as this assignment was over, she would request one. Why, she was actually yearning to become closer to a man, which would be laughable if it was anyone but Clint.

What she needed was a strong dose of reality. In other words, a trip home to visit her parents. That was a sure cure for what ailed her.

She was so lost in thought that she didn't see Raphael standing in her path until she bumped into him.

"Oh! I'm sorry, I didn't see—"

"I know. You have this delicious little frown on your pretty face. I would like to erase it for you." He touched her forehead lightly and smiled. "There. It is better, no?" He glanced past her. "And where is your ferocious watchdog this afternoon, hmm?"

"Rocky? He's probably waiting out front. Did you want to see him about something?" she asked with a saucy smile.

"Not at all. I had hoped that we could spend some time together, perhaps get to know each other a little better. Seldom have I met a woman who intrigues me as you do." His eyes lingered on the low neck of her blouse.

She had to fight the reflex that made her want to place her hand over the cleavage in the outfit she had chosen to practice in. "Rocky's very possessive, I'm afraid."

"I don't blame him in the least. If you were mine I would treat you like a rare jewel and lock you away from others who might wish to steal you."

She giggled. "You say the sweetest things, Rafe."

He handed her a card. "If you can slip away from your keeper, give me a call. I'd like to show you my place."

"Oh! You live here in Vegas?"

"Yes. It's one of several homes I have. It would give me great pleasure to show it to you."

Here was a break they weren't expecting. If she could gain access to his home, she could set up more areas that could be monitored.

"I'd like that," she said breathlessly, lowering her lashes to cover the interest in her eyes. She glanced at the card. "I'll call you if I can get away."

He looked smug at the easy conquest. "Fine. I'll be waiting for your call."

As soon as she got to the dressing room, she discovered Raphael's assistants were already there. One of them gave her a haughty look and said something in Spanish that didn't sound particularly flattering. The other one grinned but didn't reply.

Oops. Now she was making enemies of the women she'd hoped to befriend. Funny how jealousy could change the mood around a place.

She changed out of her practice clothes, which were damp from perspiration. The lights onstage heated the area until she felt as though she were in a sauna.

Once dressed, she came out to find the women had left.

No doubt they were used to Raphael's roving eye, but it wouldn't do for her to think his assistants were harmless.

Turning back to the shared dressing room, she took the opportunity to quickly go through everything they'd left there in the off chance she might discover new information. She found a small unmarked booklet that appeared to hold addresses at the bottom of a makeup bag. She stuck it into her purse to make copies and then return before the evening performance.

Gabrielle didn't see Clint when she went out front. Knowing him, he was probably checking with the crew to find out any late-breaking developments.

She stopped into the coffee shop for a quick sandwich, then returned to their rooms. Clint was standing looking out the window when she walked in. He turned when he heard the door. She smiled but he didn't respond. In fact, he did not appear to be happy at the moment.

"Look what I found," she said, holding the little book open in her hand. "I want to make copies." She moved toward her bedroom.

"Where did you find it?"

"In the dressing room, why?"

"I want to know why you agreed to go to Romero's place without discussing it with me first."

She stopped in her tracks and turned. "How did you know about that?"

"Because you went to great lengths to make sure his place has ears. He's already discussing it on the phone."

"Oh." She fiddled with her earring. "Actually I told him I'd think about it. I haven't made a commitment to him."

"Good," he said with obvious satisfaction. He walked over to the sofa and sat down. He nodded to the chair nearby and said, "Let's go over what you had in mind to do if you went with him."

She couldn't understand why she was suddenly so self-conscious with this man. She was acting like a schoolgirl with a crush. How ridiculous could she get! She walked back to the grouping of furniture that occupied the center of the room and sat down across from him.

"I thought if I could get inside, we'd have a better chance to check out his operation," she said, excited with this new opportunity.

"Not if he has you flat on your back in his bedroom," he replied tersely.

"Don't be crude."

"Then don't you be naive."

"I'm a trained operative. I can take care of myself."

"Trained or not, one wrong slip and you'll be discovered. Care to guess what your life will be worth then? I don't think the risk is worth it. We've managed to cover him more than we expected. We're already monitoring his calls—"

"But if I was actually on the premises, I might be able to search for evidence while I'm there."

"And how do you propose to explain your interest in his property to him?"

"I'll make sure he doesn't catch me."

"Use your head, will you? From the moment you walk into his place, he's going to be concentrating on you. You aren't going to have a chance to do a thing."

"All right. Then while I'm keeping him occupied, you could slip in and—"

"No way. Forget it."

"Scared, Callaway?"

"No. I don't want you keeping him occupied while I do anything, understand?"

"I could understand Rocky saying something like that, but why are you so concerned? Or maybe you don't realize that you're sounding like a jealous lover.''

He sat back as though she'd just slapped him. After a moment, he said, "I am?"

She grinned at the expression on his face. "Oh, quite definitely. I'm flattered, of course, but I really don't believe you have to worry about my virtue."

"I'm not. But there's no reason to play this so close to the edge."

"When we originally planned this we didn't expect him to notice me or to come on to me. I think we need to bring this new development under consideration. It gives us more options."

Clint got up from the sofa and began to pace, muttering to himself. Finally he said, "Maybe I'm not being objective enough on this. I don't know. Let's run it past Ken before making any final plans. I'm willing to let him decide. What about you?"

If she were honest with herself, she would admit that the last thing she wanted was to be anywhere alone with Raphael. However, if it was part of her job she was willing to do it.

"Fine. Let's talk to Ken and see what he says."

"Sounds like an unnecessary risk to me," Ken said sometime later. "According to what's coming in, we're picking up information we can act on without putting you on the premises."

"I'm also faxing copies of pages from a book in one of the girl's things. The names may have nothing to do with Raphael, but it wouldn't hurt to check them out," Gabrielle said.

"I don't like the idea that he's noticed you," Ken went on. "I think it's putting you in more danger than is called for. My plan was to have you backstage with his troupe, unobtrusively gathering information." He sounded a little irritated.

"Don't blame her," Clint said. "In those costumes you saw fit to send out here for her, she's not going to blend into the woodwork, that's for sure."

"I was told they were typical for the area."

"Yes, but Gabrielle isn't. She projects a seductive innocence that's very provocative."

Gabrielle gave him a startled glance across the expanse between them, which Clint ignored.

Ken chuckled. "You noticed, did you?"

"I'd have to be blind not to. She had the audience mesmerized last night with her singing and her appearance. We may have gotten more than we bargained for here."

"Then I'd advise not to have her go any further where Raphael's concerned."

Clint looked pleased but his voice remained even. "Glad you agree. Do you intend to arrest him out here or wait until we're out of the picture?"

"I'd prefer to wait. He's supposed to be there another three weeks. Once you're gone, there'll be no reason for him to connect you with what's going down.''

"We'll get through the rest of the week as quietly as possible," Clint said.

When they hung up, Clint looked around at Gabrielle who'd been on the bedroom phone. She got up and came toward him. "Seductive innocence?" she said with a grin. "Why, Rocky, honey, I never knew you could be so eloquent."

Clint could feel his ears turning red. "Yeah, that's me. A regular poet." He stuffed his hands into his pants pockets and frowned at her.

She walked up to him and rested her palm against his cheek. "I'm glad you're the one here with me, Clint. I've never had an assignment quite like this one before. I had no idea I would gain this type of attention."

"You're a woman with many talents, Gabrielle. I always knew you were a proficient agent. I had no idea you had the acting and singing talent to pull this off. If you don't watch out, Woody Allen will be offering you a part in his next movie."

She shook her head. "No, thanks. I think I'll stick with what I know."

"Until you decide to settle down with a family, I suppose."

"I'm a professional career woman," she said lightly. "I never intend to have a family. I'll be one of those operatives they'll have to retire when I can no longer handle the tougher assignments." She glanced at her watch. "Well, I've got to get ready to go back downstairs. Are you going down with me?"

"Yes. For the next week I intend to stick to your side like glue. Raphael won't have to wonder why you had to turn him down. He'll see you can't possibly get away from me."

She nodded and, while Clint waited, she went into her room and gathered the various items she would wear that night. He reviewed what he had just said to her and realized that he had meant every word. He didn't want her to go out of his life when this assignment was over. He didn't want to occasionally run into her at the office and go months at a time without seeing her.

Somehow he had to find a way to convince her that they could make a relationship work.

How strange. How could he have developed such an attachment to a person he barely knew? Somehow, he felt as though he'd known her forever. She needed him, whether she knew it or not. It would be up to him to convince her of that fact.

Chapter 6

The curtain rose on the last performance on Saturday night. The applause thundered at the sight of Gabrielle standing there beside the piano. The noise confirmed what she suspected—the room was filled to capacity. With the lights so high it was difficult for her to see the audience but they had made their presence known in no uncertain terms.

She was a hit.

She should be thrilled to have pulled off this particular assignment. Instead all she could feel was relief that their stay in Las Vegas was almost over.

The strain on her nerves was beginning to tell. It wasn't the actual performance causing the strain. She'd gotten used to performing in public during the past week. It was the tension between her and Clint that was taking its toll.

In public he was loverlike enough to convince the most discerning spectator, but when they were alone he'd revert to his usual aloof and abrupt manner.

She wasn't certain why he'd changed toward her. All she knew was that she was increasingly uncomfortable around him.

Tonight she sang her heart out. The words seemed to take on new meaning as she sang about "The Man That Got Away," "Blues in the Night," "St. Louis Blues," and "Summertime."

It was when she sang "Can't Help Lovin' Dat Man" that she knew what had happened to her. Somehow, someway, she'd fallen in love with Clint Callaway.

Had he noticed something in her behavior that she'd been unaware of? Was that why he'd seemed to change toward her, to withdraw?

When the last few notes died away, the silence left in the room was suddenly shattered with another wave of deafening applause. Gabrielle smiled and bowed, but when the clamoring continued she looked at her accompanist with confusion.

He began to play the notes of another song they'd practiced, and the audience finally quietened to hear her encore. It was an old Gershwin tune, "Someone to Watch Over Me," and she found herself once again caught up in its message. By the time she finished, she knew that she'd never sung so well or with so much heartfelt emotion.

This time she left the stage as soon as the song ended and ran directly into Clint who stood just offstage. Without a word he pulled her into his arms and kissed her with a devastating intensity. She couldn't have been more surprised. Was this part of the performance? Was someone backstage watching them?

Regardless of his motive, she allowed herself to relax against him, and returned his kiss with unabashed passion. Some small part of her realized they were standing just offstage, in the way of the next group preparing to go on. She could hear whispers and snickers, but she didn't care.

When he finally relaxed his hold on her, she sighed.

"Let's get you out of that outfit before you catch cold," he murmured in a husky voice.

He waited outside the dressing room door. She was shaking so hard she had difficulty removing the stage makeup and unfastening her dress. What was happening between them? Why was she having such vivid dreams of making love to him? How could her subconscious be so full of images that were unlike anything she'd ever experienced?

There had been times during the past few days when she'd wondered if she was losing her mind.

She'd chosen to wear her most conservative outfit tonight, which was still a far cry from the suits she was used to. This dress had a mandarin collar and a long skirt, if she ignored the slit up the side that stopped about midthigh.

When she opened the door Clint gave her a brief, comprehensive glance before draping his arm around her shoulders. They walked toward the door that led into the casino. Just before they reached the casino entrance the back door that lead to the parking lot flew open. Two men stood there blocking the way, with pistols trained on them.

"You're to come with us," one of them said. "This way."

There was a black limousine pulled up next to the doorway with the rear door open.

Clint gave Gabrielle's shoulders a squeeze. "What's with the strong-arm tactics, guys? Why don't you just ask us to go with you?"

"Get inside," the other one said.

Clint helped Gabrielle to get inside the back of the limo. The driver didn't turn his head, continuing to gaze straight ahead. The two men got in and sat across from them. They'd put their pistols away.

Clint held Gabrielle's hand. "Care to tell us where we're going?"

"You'll know soon enough."

"I think you fellows have been watching too many gangster movies. Come on, what's this all about?"

"Just shut up."

Clint settled back in his seat, hoping he'd shown enough concern. He wanted them to think he'd been surprised, when the truth was Romero's plans had been picked up by one of the bugs they'd planted. Gabrielle's suggestion to get someone inside of Romero's house had been a good one, so one of their operatives had gone in earlier in the day as part of the cleaning crew that worked there each week.

Clint had discussed the plan with Ken since he had no way of warning Gabrielle ahead of time. Romero's plan was to grab Gabrielle without giving her any choice in the matter. Clint had found the slimeball's attitude toward a woman he professed to be attracted to a little primitive. As soon as he got off the phone with Ken, Clint never let Gabrielle out of his sight. He'd made certain he was with her every moment except for when she was onstage or changing clothes.

Clint was looking forward to finding out how Romero would handle having him along for the ride.

He'd ended up not telling Gabrielle what to expect, and he knew when she found out that he'd had some advance notice that she would be furious with him. He could have used the excuse that he hadn't had time, but the kiss they had shared made that lie obvious.

They had to figure out what Romero was up to, and it didn't really matter to him how angry Gabrielle became. He wanted her alive. She could yell at him all she wanted once this thing was over.

The limousine paused in front of a gated home while the driver spoke into a hand-held device. The gates swung open and the car proceeded inside the grounds of a spacious mansion. If this was Romero's place, he certainly wasn't disguising his wealth from anyone.

Once inside the house, the two men directed Clint and Gabrielle into a formal living area. The men left them in the room and disappeared.

"Nice place, huh?" he asked in a cocky tone of voice. Gabrielle looked at him sharply, then smiled.

"Why can't you get us a place like this, Rocky? I try real hard to earn money for us."

"I'm workin' on it, baby. Give me some time. I have a few deals going as we speak. Didn't I promise you if you stuck with me that you'd have everything your little ol' heart desires?"

Romero spoke from the open doorway. "So I will have two for dinner, I see. Perhaps it's just as well." He walked over to Gabrielle and took both her hands, holding them as he openly admired the way she looked. "We're going to have to do something about your watchdog, don't you think?"

"Well, Rocky's been taking care of me for a long time, Rafe. He's a good man."

"Whatever you say. In the meantime, may I offer you a drink?"

"Not for me. Thanks," she said.

He looked at Clint with a raised brow. "Got any beer?" Clint asked.

Romero went over to a wet bar and opened the small refrigerator there. He found a beer and poured it into a glass, handing it to Clint without speaking.

"Thanks."

"Shall I show you to your room?" he asked Gabrielle, ignoring Clint.

"My room? I really can't stay here, you know. It's sweet of you to offer, but—"

"We've made other plans," Clint said. "I don't know what this is all about, but you should know by now that we're a team. One of us doesn't go anywhere without the other."

"I see. That could put a slight crimp in my plans, then. You see, I intend to marry Ms. Grant. I think she'll see that I have a great deal more to offer than you can possibly give her."

"Sorry, pal, but you're a little late. Me and Gabrielle are already married."

"Nonsense. I had the records checked and—"

"Not under our real names." He reached into the breast pocket of his coat, glad that the team had had the foresight to have a license forged. All the equipment they'd been outfitted with had come in handy. "Here." He offered it to Romero.

The man took it and unfolded the paper, studying it carefully. "This shows you were married this week."

Clint grinned. "Yeah. We figured as long as we were in Vegas, we might as well tie the knot."

"Then allow me to congratulate you. I had hoped that— Ah, well, I suppose it doesn't matter." He turned to Gabrielle. "Do you intend to continue with your career?"

"Of course."

"Mmm. Then perhaps I can still assist you." He glanced at Clint from the corner of his eye. "Perhaps in time you'll see that you may have made the wrong choice. In the meantime, you'll be my guests overnight."

"Now what?" Gabrielle asked Clint as soon as they were left alone in a large bedroom.

"We wait until morning. Either he lets us return to the hotel or I signal the boys on that handy-dandy little watch you're wearing to come knocking on the door. One way or the other, we'll be out of here by morning."

She glanced at the bed in the room. "In the meantime, I suppose you expect us to share that bed?"

"I'll be a perfect gentleman. I promise."

"This hasn't worked out quite as we planned."

"At least you aren't here alone."

"Where did you get the marriage license?"

"Ken had it made up on the off chance we could make use of it."

"This place gives me the creeps," she said, walking over to the window and looking outside. "There are men with dogs patrolling the area."

"Somehow that doesn't surprise me."

She turned and looked at him. "You don't seem worried."

"No need to be. Everything's under control."

There was a tap on the door. Clint went over and opened it. A young woman stood there. "I'm to show you to the dining room," she said, smiling.

"Great. I could use a little something to eat. How about you?" he asked Gabrielle.

"Actually it's been a rather long day for me. I'd prefer to get some sleep."

"Not without me, honey. I intend to stick to you like glue, remember?"

The meal was tense. Gabrielle spoke in monosyllables.

"Look, Romero," Clint finally said. "We'd much prefer to spend the rest of the night at our hotel. We've got another long day ahead of us tomorrow, as you know."

"You can leave anytime you like," Raphael replied. "However, I want Gabrielle to stay."

"No way. We're a matched set."

Raphael sighed. "You're a very stubborn man."

"I've heard that a few times before."

With sudden decision, Raphael said, "All right. You win. It is obvious Gabrielle's exhausted. I didn't mean to frighten you, my dear," he said to her, his voice softening. "I wanted a chance to get to know you better, to allow us both a chance to learn more about each other."

"Perhaps some other time," she said in a low voice. Clint couldn't tell if she was acting or not. She really did look exhausted.

It was almost three o'clock in the morning by the time they arrived back at the hotel. As soon as they reached their rooms, Clint put in a call to the team. By the time he hung up, he was no longer expecting to get much rest that night.

"He's pulling out," he told Gabrielle as soon as he hung up the phone. "Something's scared him. I think he planned to take you with him, then changed his mind when I showed up."

"What does Ken expect us to do?"

"We're out of it now. He wants us to catch the first available flight out of here. You've just had the shortest successful career in the history of show business."

She started toward her bedroom. "It was fun while it lasted, I suppose, but I'm more than ready to get back to work in my own clothes. Give me half an hour and I'll be ready to leave."

Chapter 7

Two months had passed since his assignment in Las Vegas before Clint finally got the courage to call Gabrielle at her home. She answered on the third ring, sounding breathless.

"Hope I'm not interrupting something," he said as a number of possible activities she could have been involved in, which would cause her to sound that way, immediately flashed into his mind. He didn't like the idea of any of them.

"Clint?"

"Uh, yeah. It's me."

"Oh . . . well . . . this is a surprise."

"Are you busy?"

"No. I'd just gotten into the shower when I thought I heard my phone."

He had a sudden vision of her standing there without clothes on. His body immediately responded to the thought. "Oops. Sorry about that. Let me call you back."

"Oh, it's okay. I grabbed a towel and I'm dried off now." She paused, and when he didn't say anything, she prodded. "This is the first time you've called me at home."

"I know. I, uh, well, I've been gone most of the time since we got back from Vegas."

"Congratulations on nailing Raphael."

"Thanks in large part to you. Those addresses you found were a big help. They gave us the cities where we could focus our attention. Since they weren't on his entertainment circuit, we hadn't investigated those areas."

She was quiet for a while before she said, "We were just lucky Raphael didn't try something the night he took us to his home. For a while I thought he'd discovered our identities."

"No, we were listening too closely for that to have come about without some warning. I think he was counting on getting you away from me long enough to dazzle you with his riches. He really didn't expect me to be there. When it came right down to it, he wasn't willing to risk bodily injury to seduce a woman. I must have convinced him I was serious about protecting you.''

"He never found out we were the ones who managed to get the necessary information to arrest him, then?''

"Nope."

"That's good." There was another lengthy pause between them. Finally she said, "It was nice of you to call me with an update on the matter."

"That isn't why I called."

"Oh?"

"No. I—uh, well, I'd like to talk to you if you have the time available."

"About what?" she asked cautiously.

"I'd prefer to explain in person. Maybe you'd like to have dinner with me tomorrow night."

"You mean as in a date for dinner?"

"Well . . . yeah. I guess that's what I'm saying."

"I don't think that would be a very good idea, Clint. I've always made it a rule not to date any colleague of mine." As though afraid he'd take her rejection the wrong way, she hurriedly went on, "Please understand it isn't just you. It would be anyone I work with."

"Actually I've always had a similar rule. The thing is, I really would like to talk to you sometime."

"I tell you what, why don't you come to my place tomorrow night? I'll prepare something simple to eat and we'll have privacy to discuss whatever's on your mind. Is it something about this case?''

"Uh, not exactly. I'll explain tomorrow night. What time would be convenient for you?''

"Seven or thereabouts."

"Great. See you then."

Clint hung up the phone wondering if he'd finally fallen off the edge of sanity and was now drifting in a fantasy world. All he knew at the moment was that he had to see Gabrielle again. He had to talk to her. He had to tell her what he'd been going through.

She'd probably confirm the fact that he was crazy. He certainly couldn't argue with her about that.

"You're very prompt," she said the following night when she opened the door. "C'mon in. I wasn't very imaginative with our meal. Hope you don't mind."

He noted that she was in slacks and a short-sleeved sweater. She had her hair pulled away from her face but it still fell in curls down to her shoulders. She looked wonderful to him. God, but he'd missed her.

He'd definitely dressed down. He wore a pair of jeans that were almost faded to white, they'd been washed so many times. He also wore one of his comfortable Western-style shirts and boots. He wanted her to get to know him, who he really was, not just the agent or Rocky, her possessive lover.

He stepped into the apartment and immediately caught the mouth-watering aroma of something delicious in the oven. "Smells good in here," he heard himself say. Now that was an original line.

The truth was that he couldn't remember a time when he'd been so nervous. So much depended on how he presented his case to her. He was suffering from stage fright, something that never happened to him. But then, he'd never faced anything quite so important to him before.

"Dinner should be ready in another twenty minutes or so. Would you like something to drink?"

"I don't suppose you have any beer, do you?"

She grinned. "As a matter of fact, I picked up some today. I found a Texas brand I thought you might like." She went behind the bar that separated the kitchen from the living room. "Sit down and make yourself comfortable."

He sat down. If only he could make himself relax. He'd never felt so much on edge, even during his most dangerous assignments.

She brought him a tall glass of beer, then sat down across from him, an inquiring expression on her face.

He drank half the glass before he cleared his throat and said, "I know what I'm going to say is going to sound strange, but I have to ask you something."

"Okay," she said slowly, watching him with obvious curiosity.

He couldn't think of what to say. "I don't know where to start," he finally muttered, then drank another long swallow of beer.

"I'm afraid I can't help you, Clint. I haven't the foggiest notion of what you're trying to say."

"Have you ever had a nagging voice in your head prompting you to do something and it won't leave you alone?" She looked even more puzzled so he tried to be a little more clear. "I mean, your conscience or something like that. Well, that's what I've been going through since we left Las Vegas."

"Your conscience has been bothering you?"

"Yes. I mean, no. It's not exactly my conscience but something sure as hell is keeping me awake nights. And when I dream, I dream the same things over and over."

"About Las Vegas?"

"About you."

She stared at him in astonishment, obviously speechless. The oven timer chose that particular moment to go off. He wasn't sure if he was being saved by the bell or whether she would decide to take back her invitation for dinner and show him the door.

Gabrielle got up at the sound of the buzzer and hurried to the kitchen. She turned off the oven and pulled out the casserole, setting it on top of the stove to cool. Opening the refrigerator door, she pulled out two salads and set them on the bar.

"I told you it wasn't much," she said apologetically.

He jumped up from the sofa as though propelled by an unseen spring and strode to the bar. "This looks great, Gabrielle. Honestly. I can't remember the last time I had a home-cooked meal."

She dished up the casserole onto two plates and set one in front of him. "Sit down. We'll eat, then maybe we can get back to our discussion."

As if he could eat anything while waiting to get her reaction. But she was right. There was no sense in letting good food go to waste. As soon as he had his first bite, he forgot all about his nonexistent appetite, eventually having seconds.

By the time the dishes were rinsed and in the dishwasher he was more calm. Maybe he could make more sense this time.

They sat down once again—he on the sofa, she in a nearby chair. He leaned forward, resting his elbows on his knees.

"Here's the thing. Since our week together in Las Vegas, I can't get you out of my mind." He held up his hand when she started to say something. "Please. Let me get this out in one piece. I've tried to forget you. Believe me, I have tried. But there's this little nagging voice in my head that keeps saying things like, 'Why don't you phone her? Why don't you tell her how you feel?' That's why I called last night. I figured nothing could be worse than listening to that annoying voice prompting me to make a complete fool of myself."

She watched him carefully. "How would you do that?"

"Because I want to marry you and I don't know how to go about asking you," he blurted out. "There. I've said it. I know all the reasons why you're going to say no. We work together, for one. If we don't believe in dating a fellow agent, where does that put marrying one on the forbidden list? I know you intend not to marry because you never want to be in a situation like your mother's. As a matter of fact, I never thought I would want to—"

"What did you say?" she asked urgently, leaning toward him with a ferocious frown on her face.

"What part didn't you get?" he replied irritably. This was the most awkward situation he'd ever been in.

"You mentioned my mother."

"Oh. Well, yeah. I understand why your childhood would have turned you off to the whole idea of marriage, but ours wouldn't have to be that way. I mean—"

With frost coating each word she asked, "How do you know about my childhood and my mother?"

He stared at her blankly for several moments. "You told me," he finally said. Puzzled by her reaction, he asked, "Didn't you?"

She got up from her chair and walked across the room, away from him. When she turned, her features had been wiped clean of all expression. "I have never told a soul about my family, or my childhood. No one. Not my friends in school, not my roommate at college, nor anyone with whom I've worked. Including you."

"Then how would I know about it?" he asked reasonably.

"You must have looked at my personnel files or something. You must have—"

"Whoa, now. Just wait a minute. I would never attempt to find out more about you than what you wanted me to know. Besides, how you felt watching your mother struggle to care for a large family certainly wouldn't be on any report about you, now would it?"

"Then how could you possibly know how I feel about my mother or marriage?"

"Exactly my point. You must have told me."

"When?"

"Hell, I don't know." He got up, running his hand through his hair. "I can't believe we're having this conversation. I thought your feelings about marriage were a given. What I'm trying to do is to convince you to give marriage a chance...with me."

Her eyes widened as he approached her. She took a quick step backward. "I don't need to be reminded of how I react to you, Clint Callaway. So keep your distance. It's just a childish crush, that's all."

"You think I have a crush on you?" he asked, his tone filled with patent disbelief.

"Of course not. I'm talking about me! It was just the situation we were in, that's all. Pretending to be lovers, waking up in your bed like that, your being so possessive around Raphael. Given enough time I know I'll forget all of that—"

"Waking up in my bed! What are you talking about?"

She covered her mouth with her hand as though to stop the words from pouring out, but of course it was too late. "Nothing. It was nothing. Really. I was probably overtired that night . . . probably got up in the middle of the night and became disoriented."

"You were in my bed?"

"Just once. After that, I made certain to lock my door in case it happened again. I've never been aware of any sleepwalking tendencies before, but—"

He placed his hands on her shoulders. "Gabrielle, honey. Would you just shut up for a minute? It's okay, whatever happened, don't you see? It doesn't matter how I know about your feelings toward marriage. I just do. Maybe subconsciously you were drawn to me in the same way I'm drawn to you. Maybe we're supposed to be together on a permanent basis. Have you ever thought about that?"

"No," she replied, her voice shaking. "It would never work. We couldn't possibly..." She stopped talking and looked him straight in the eye. "I want you so badly I ache with it. I dream about making love to you. I wake up in the morning miserable to discover it was only a dream. I don't know what to do anymore." Tears filled her eyes.

For the first time in a long time, Clint knew that things were going to work out all right. Maybe his conscience or his subconscious or some guardian angel somewhere had been right to nag him until he put his fears aside and approached her with his feelings.

"I know exactly what to do. And we're going to do it right now."

"This really feels strange," she said several hours later.

"In what way?" he asked.

"I feel as though we've done this before. Here we are in Las Vegas, just married, and we're having dinner in our suite." She looked at the sparkling ring on her finger that matched the one on his. "I feel as though I'm going to wake up and find that I've been dreaming again."

"You know what they say about déjà vu. I guess it really happens, sometimes." He reached across the small table and took her hand. "Except this time it's real. When I wake up later this morning I want you lying beside me. You won't be sleepwalking this time. I promise you that."

He picked her up and carried her into the bedroom.

"I guess your brother is really going to tease you about being the first one to get married, after all."

"My brother? How do you know about my brother?"

PART II
Cade

Chapter 8

Cade Callaway was hot, tired and dusty when he finally returned to the ranch house for lunch. He'd been out since daybreak, trying to stay ahead of repairs on the place.

Of course he had ranch hands to do the work, but he'd long since discovered that they worked a hell of a lot faster when he was part of the crew.

Now all he wanted was to clean up and sit down to several gallons of iced tea and a good hot meal. Thank God for the Ramirez family. The mother and daughter kept the house clean and him fed, while the father and two sons worked on the ranch.

Without the women, he'd probably starve to death and live in a pigsty.

After a quick shower and a fresh change of clothes, another blessing from the Ramirez ladies, Cade trotted downstairs to eat. Maria stopped him before he could sit down.

"Matt called. He said to have you call him as soon as you came in."

"Surely I can have lunch first."

She shrugged. "That's just what he said."

"The world won't come to an end if I don't call him until after I eat. Besides, whatever he has to say can be better dealt with on a full stomach. I have a hunch I know why he's calling."

Maria disappeared into the kitchen and came back with a steaming plate of enchiladas, tacos, Spanish rice and refried beans. She also had a plate of steaming corn tortillas, no doubt freshly made.

By the time he finished eating, Cade's mood had improved appreciably. He whistled as he strode down the hallway to his office and put in the call to his cousin in San Antonio.

As soon as he heard Matt's voice, Cade said, "So, what's up?" He propped his booted feet on the desk and leaned back in his chair.

"Plenty, my friend. I'm going to need you in town for the next few weeks. Think you can handle that?"

"What for? You're the lawyer, not me."

"But you're the one who'll be testifying if we're going to defend against this water rights lawsuit. The other side wants to take your deposition at the last minute."

"I thought trial was set in three weeks?"

"It is. But they're getting a little nervous. They want to hear what you have to say. Plus, I need your help in identifying some of the maps and plats that will make up part of our exhibits."

"This whole situation is ridiculous. This ranch has been in the family for generations. Why do they think they can come in now and give us a bad time over our rights to the water and underground minerals on the property?"

"Because it's a free country. A person can sue if they think there's a chance of collecting anything off of it. Right now, water is one of the most precious commodities along the Texas-Mexico border. If they can show a valid claim to any part of the water on the ranch, they stand to make big money, either by getting you to buy them off or by reselling the rights to someone else."

"Which is the bottom line, isn't it?" Cade said with disgust. "The name Callaway means money to lots of people. I suppose they feel we'd rather pay them some kind of settlement than go to trial. At least this particular group is going to learn we don't operate that way."

"Well, if you want me to successfully defend this case, I'm going to need your help. You know more about the history of the place than anyone else in the family.''

Cade sighed. ''I suppose that's true. At least while the older generation is busy gallivanting all over Ireland. It would serve 'em all right if we told them to be here for the trial.''

''Dad thought we should handle it without them and I agree. There's no point in riling everybody for no good reason,'' Matt said.

''Is Candy still working on this case with you?''

Cade heard Matt groan at his question and grinned at the sound. Matt knew it wasn't just casual curiosity at work.

''Yes, Cade, Candy is still working on this one with me,'' Matt replied with a hint of asperity.

''Good. Let me talk to her.''

''Damn it, Cade, when are you going to give up on that one? With all the women out there falling all over you, why do you insist on chasing after the one female who's not impressed with either you or your charm?''

''She'll come around. Give me time.''

''You've been asking her out for over two years. I don't see where you've made much headway.''

''Sure I have. She no longer crosses herself whenever I walk into her office. And once I think I saw her almost smile when she first caught sight of me.''

Matt laughed. ''It was probably just gas. Look, Cade, I've got to get back to work. Get up here as soon as you can. You can stay at my place if you'd like. I've gotta go."

"Don't hang up! I want Candy, remember?"

Matt laughed. "You sound like a kid, you know. Just remember that you can't have everything you want, okay?"

"Maybe not, but I've always enjoyed a challenge."

There were several clicks on the line, then a very professional-sounding voice said, "This is Candace Monroe. May I help you?"

"Hi, Candy-cane. Have you missed me?"

He heard a definite groan in his ear. "What do you want, Cade? I'm very busy at the moment."

"Is that any way to greet the man you're going to marry someday?" When she didn't respond he said, "Hello? Are you still there?"

"What do you want, Cade?" she repeated in measured tones.

"Well, it looks as if I'm needed in town, so I thought I'd check to see if you'd like to have dinner with me tonight."

"No, thank you. Is there anything else?"

"You tryin' to break my heart, honey?" he drawled. "How can you be so cold to me?"

"Actually, it's quite easy. I'm certain you won't have any trouble finding feminine companionship tonight, Cade. If that's all, I've really got to go."

Candy hung up the phone and discovered that her hand was trembling. That man could make her angrier than anyone she'd ever known. Didn't he understand the word 'no'?

She had never once shown him the slightest bit of encouragement since she'd joined the law firm run by Cameron and Matthew Callaway. At least *they* treated her with courtesy and respect, despite the fact they were Callaways, too. Otherwise she would have left after six months.

The thought of Cade coming into town made her groan with dread. Of course she'd known he would have to come in soon. The trial was rapidly approaching and she and Matt would need Cade's help.

She turned away from the phone and saw that Matt was watching her from the doorway.

"Hi. Did you need something?" she asked, smiling. She liked Matt. He was only five years older than she, but immeasurably older in life experience.

Matt sat down across the desk from her. "I take it your conversation with Cade didn't go well."

She took a deep breath and audibly exhaled. "That man is impossible, do you know that? Absolutely impossible. It's hard to believe you're both Callaways."

"I may carry the name, but he's from the true bloodline."

"I've met your dad and his brothers and they are gentlemen in the finest sense of the word. Cade, on the other hand, is an egotistical jerk. I'm sorry if I've offended you, Matt, but he is."

"Don't apologize. He is who he is. Actually I've never seen Cade so intent on pursuing a woman before. It's usually the other way around. You should be flattered that he keeps coming back despite your attitude."

"Oh, spare me, please. Flattered? Hah! Cade Callaway is rude, crude and—" She searched for a withering description. "And perfectly obnoxious!"

Matt grinned. "There, you see? The man's obviously good at something, isn't he?"

"Are you actually taking up for him?"

"I just think you're being a little hard on him, that's all. All he wants is to take you to dinner sometime, or so he tells me."

"And you believe that, of course?"

"Is there some reason why I shouldn't?"

"I think he's making a career out of seeing how many women he can get into his bed! You can't pick up a newspaper that there isn't some mention of that man attending this function or that function with some good-looking woman. Invariably he's with a different one every photo. Not that they don't all have a similar appearance. He's obviously attracted to the 3-B's type of woman."

"Which is?"

"Blond-buxom-bimbo."

"Ouch. You certainly don't consider yourself either a blonde or a bimbo, do you?"

Since Candy's hair shade was considered a dark auburn, she didn't need to reply to the hair color question. As far as the rest of her, she had an okay figure, but she certainly wasn't voluptuous. And since she'd graduated from law school in the top ten percent of her class, she had no need to defend her intelligence.

"My point, exactly. I'm not his type. The only reason he persists in asking me out is because I keep refusing to be seen with him. I don't want to be known as one of his groupies."

"The thrill of the chase. Is that what it is?"

"Something like that. Yes."

"Then the obvious thing for you to do is to go out with him, pretend to be enamored by him, and he'll leave you alone." Matt started to laugh when he saw the look on her face. "All right," he said, getting up from his chair. "I won't try to change your mind about Cade, but I do expect you to work with him while he's here. I've asked him to stay in town until the trial's over. I'm going to give him one of the vacant offices so he'll have a place to go through our files while he's here."

"I have no problem with the idea of working with him on a professional basis."

"I'm glad to hear it. This is an important case, Candy. We can't afford to lose it."

"I understand, Matt."

She watched him walk out of the office before she went back to work, but she kept having trouble concentrating. Cade Callaway's grinning face kept appearing on the page she was trying to read.

What was the matter with her, anyway? She had never been in a situation quite like this one before. There had been times in her life when she'd been approached by a man whom she wasn't interested in dating and her polite refusal was all that it took for him to disappear from her life.

As long as she worked in the Callaway law firm, she would be, by necessity, dealing with various members of the Callaway family. So why couldn't she accept that Cade was a notorious flirt and just ignore the man?

She was certain he came on to every woman he met the same way he did her—full of effortless charm and good will. He was good-looking, she would give him that, but that was a genetic gift that had nothing to do with the man, himself.

Maybe she reacted to him because he'd always had everything in life come far too easily for him. Granted he was a hard-worker, as Matt had pointed out to her on more than one occasion. He knew a great deal about ranching, had won several awards back in the days when he was following the rodeo circuit, and seemed to be knowledgeable about the history of the family.

It was that last part that had caused him to get involved with this lawsuit. She could handle working with him. After all, she was a professional. She was used to dealing with difficult people. What she had to remember was not to allow his silly remarks to get to her. He made them in order to get a reaction from her.

Well, from now on he was going to be disappointed. She would treat him like any other client, regardless of how outrageous he was.

Candy closed the file. Since she wasn't getting much out of reading it at the moment, she'd take a break. They still had three weeks to prepare. That would give her plenty of time.

She forced Cade Callaway out of her mind and went down the hallway to get a cup of coffee.

Chapter 9

The door to Candy's office swung open the following morning and she glanced up. As soon as she saw who stood there, she fought to control her expression.

"Good morning, Cade. How may I help you?"

"Well, now, honey-bunch, I can think of all kinds of ways, but I doubt that you'd agree to any of them," Cade replied, sauntering into the office. He immediately sprawled into one of the chairs, his long legs stretched out in front of him.

She met his amused gaze with a calmness she did not feel. "Have you spoken to Matt this morning?"

"Yes, ma'am, I have. He showed me the cubby-hole where I'm supposed to look through boxes of papers that have been dug up here and yonder. He said you'd know which ones I should go through first."

"Yes, of course. I'll show them to you." She got up and walked around her desk, but her progress was stopped by his legs blocking the way to the door. "Really, Cade, you're acting rather juvenile, don't you think?"

"Am I?" he said, slowly coming to his feet. "I suppose that's one way to look at it. Of course another way is to acknowledge that there's nothing I hate more than to be cooped up inside a building for any length of time. Now Matt's telling me I have to work here in the office with the two of you until we go to trial. I'm willing to do that, you understand, because somebody has to, and the folks don't need to be bothered with litigation. But the way I see it, you're going to be another little glitch in this whole thing."

"Me? What are you talking about?"

"Without your cooperation, my job here is going to be a lot tougher, since Matt expects us to work so closely together and all. Of course he assured me that you're a professional and will be able to ignore the strong emotions I stir within you whenever I'm around, but I'm not as convinced as he is."

Candy could feel her cheeks flaming. From temper, not from embarrassment. She forced herself to remain silent until she had firm control over her voice. When she spoke, her voice was modulated to an even tone.

"Then let me add my assurances, Cade. I *am* a professional and I want to win this case as much as you and Matt do. Therefore, you can count on me to cooperate with you fully."

They now stood about a foot apart. She felt at a distinct disadvantage, having to look up at him this close. She'd probably end up with a crick in her neck, but she refused to be the first one to look away.

He cocked an eyebrow at her. "Are you real certain about that, ma'am? One look at me just now and you were ready to call security. Since I haven't a clue what I've ever done to get your back up, I'm not sure how to negotiate a truce with you. But if you'd be so kind as to tell me what it is about me that irritates you so, I'll do my best to correct it."

Sincerity dripped like syrup from each and every word he spoke. What a crock. That "I'm just a country boy" line might work on some people, but not on her. She happened to know that he was highly educated and had a keen business sense that he kept hidden with his "aw shucks" attitude.

Candy leaned against the front of her desk and folded her arms. "All right, I will. All I ask of you is that you start treating me as you would any other colleague, not as the object of your smart-ass remarks. I'm not impressed with your manly strut, your cocky self-assurance that you are God's gift to the female population, or your adolescent need to bed every woman you meet between the ages of eighteen and thirty.''

Cade slowly drew himself up to his full height, which was considerable. "I resent that," he replied, drawling the words.

She tilted her head slightly. "Oh? What part, exactly?''

"I don't want to bed *every* woman I meet. Some of them I just enjoy having intellectually stimulating conversations with.''

"Of course you do," she agreed lightly. "Tell me, Cade, what do you do, swap copies of the latest *Literary Review* with them?''

He grinned and stuck his hands into his back pockets. "Tacky, tacky." He studied her in the silence that fell between them, then slowly nodded. "All right. If that's the way you want it. From now on I'll show you the same respect I would a woman of the cloth," he vowed solemnly.

"I can live with that just fine." She glanced at her watch. "If you'll come with me, I'll show you those files.''

He ambled along behind her to a storage room, where she pointed out the ones she wanted him to go through, then helped him carry them to the office he'd been assigned.

It *was* small, she'd give him that. He would have claustrophobia in no time. "Well," she said, dusting her hands. "I'll leave you to it. This isn't the only case I'm working on at the moment, you know."

He looked at the row of boxes on the floor, then at her. "Really? Well, as much as I wanted this opportunity to allow you to get to know me better, I really had other things planned for these next few weeks, myself. I guess we all do what we have to do."

"Yes, well—then I can count on you to treat me as though I was one of your colleagues and not somebody to flirt with?"

He grinned. "Until I can no longer fight the irresistible attraction you hold for me and I'm forced to grab you and kiss you until you acknowledge that I'm the only man you could possibly love."

Her retreat was automatic. She felt foolish when he burst out laughing. Damn him, anyway, and his ridiculous sense of humor. "Try to restrain yourself, Cade. Otherwise, you may discover my retaliation is more powerful than your attraction."

She retreated to her office, feeling as though, despite having the last word, that Cade had won that round.

The only man that she could possibly love, indeed!

"Don't you ever go home?" Candy asked Cade when she paused by his office door three days later. Cade had been there when she left the night before. It had been past eight o'clock, then. It was now a little after seven in the morning. She was used to coming in early and getting a head start on her day. What she wasn't used to was finding someone else in the office at that hour.

Cade glanced up from the papers he was studying and focused on Candy. "I've been home. I'm back." His smile was pure seduction. "If you want to check out my after-shave, feel free. It's fresh."

"Thanks, but I'll pass," she responded dryly, coming closer. "What are you working on?"

"Preparing myself for depositions scheduled for this morning. Once that's behind us, trial preparation should ease up a little."

Candy sat down in one of the chairs across from him. "I have to tell you that you've surprised me with your dedication here at the office this week. From your remarks when you got here, I didn't figure you for an office type."

Cade leaned back in his chair and placed his hands behind his neck. "I'm not. I wouldn't want to think that I had to spend the rest of my life doing this kind of work, but I don't mind helping out for a good cause." He grinned at her. "Besides, it gives me a chance to spend some time with you. I've enjoyed being able to see you every day."

She rolled her eyes. "Oh, please. It's too early in the morning for that kind of stuff."

"You think I'm kidding?"

She eyed him thoughtfully. He was really good. She had to admit it. That slightly hurt tone was a masterful touch. She folded her arms and lightly tapped her toe on the floor. "Here's what I think, Mr. Callaway. I think you go on autopilot whenever a woman's around. The charm automatically begins to ooze from every pore. It probably comes so naturally to you, you're not even aware you're doing it."

He stared at her in patent disbelief. "You'd prefer that I talked rough and tough, maybe a little crude? That turns you on, does it?"

"No. I'll tell you what turns me on. A sense of sincerity together with a great deal of integrity."

"And you think I have neither?"

"Obviously you have the integrity to operate within the framework of family expectation. But sincerity? I don't think you have a clue what it's all about."

"Why do you think that? Because I find you attractive and make no bones about it?"

"Ah, but you find every woman you meet attractive. You see her as a potential meal to feast on, then move on to another one. You have no discrimination."

"Whew! And just how did you get to be such an expert on me?"

"I've watched you operate since I first came to work here. You're very predictable, you know."

"All right. You win."

"Win what?"

"I will continue to treat you the same way I treat Matt and the other attorneys in the office. No compliments, no innuendos. I'll leave off the flirting and teasing."

She laughed, truly amused. "Impossible."

He sat up and leaned his forearms on the desk. "Want to put a little wager on it?"

She unfolded her arms and straightened her spine. "What in the world would that be?"

"Let's set a time limit. We're going to be working together on a daily basis until this trial is over. Say, for the next two weeks—or whenever we conclude this case—if I do anything or say anything that you can interpret as being insincere and oozing with charm—your words, I believe—then I will pay for you to spend a romantic weekend wherever you'd like to go with the person of your choice."

"Two weeks, or when this case is concluded?"

"That's right."

"You couldn't last for two days."

"So is it a deal?"

Now she was a little uneasy. There must be a catch, even if she couldn't quite see it at the moment. "What if you manage by some miracle to pull it off?"

"Then you have to pay for the same kind of weekend for me."

"Hmm."

"What's that supposed to mean?"

"This sounds too easy not to be a trick of some kind."

"Nope. It's all there, starting right now. You can put it in writing if you'd like."

She stood and extended her hand to him. "Fine. I'll accept the wager. I've been needing to get away for some time now. I already know where I'll go...to the Virgin Islands."

He took her hand and formally shook it.

"If you have time," he said briskly, "I'd like to go over with you some of the possible questions I may be asked at the depositions this morning."

Candy blinked at the change in the man before her. He'd become polite but aloof...all business. With just a few words, his tone and attitude had changed. Was it possible that the flirtatious, outrageous man she thought she knew, the man whom she disliked so intensely, was merely a persona that didn't reflect the true man?

It was going to be interesting to find out.

"Let me get my notes and I'll go over them with you," she said. He nodded without looking up and she left the office, a little disoriented by the change she'd just witnessed.

One thing she had to admit, if to no other person than herself, there was never a dull moment when Cade Callaway was around.

* * *

It was Friday afternoon before the trial began on Monday. Matt poked his head around Candy's door and said, "Have you seen Cade?"

"Oh! I forgot to tell you. He got a call about some kind of problem at the ranch just before lunch. He said he'd go out and deal with it, stay the night and be back here first thing tomorrow morning."

"Ah." Matt came in and sat down across from Candy. "That will be soon enough for what I need, I suppose." He watched her for a moment, then asked, "So how has it been going for you with Cade in the office?"

She glanced up from the court files she was preparing and said, "Fine."

"No. Really."

"I'm telling you, it's been fine," she replied with exasperation. "Actually he's been treating me like I was his maiden aunt, if such a person existed."

Matt laughed. "As a matter of fact, we used to have a maiden aunt, although she was actually our great-aunt. Good ol' Aunt Letty. Story has it that she practically raised the three boys—Cole, my dad Cameron and Cody—when their parents were killed."

Candy leaned back in her chair and smiled. "You don't say. Somehow it's hard for me to picture your dad and his brothers being influenced by a maiden aunt."

"She was a tough old bird, I'll give you that. Wouldn't take any nonsense off of anyone. Of course, by the time I joined the family she'd simmered down some. She was a family institution, all right."

"I take it she's no longer living."

Matt nodded. "We always thought she was too stubborn to lie down and die, so it caught all of us by surprise. The doctor said her heart just gave out one day. She'd complained of feeling tired and went to her room for a nap. Since she was at least eighty-five at the time, no one thought much about it. They found her an hour or so later."

"Then it was very peaceful, her going?"

"I suppose. The ranch never seemed the same without her bossing everybody around, though. She was really a character." He paused and looked at her. "You know, I think Aunt Letty would have really liked you."

"Me? What are you talking about?"

"Well, you remind me of her, in a way."

"Well, thanks a lot! A tough old bird, I believe you said?"

"Not that part particularly, but you're very straight with people, you don't play games and if I might be so bold, you have your share of pride and stubbornness."

She grinned. "You bet I do. Otherwise, I would never have made it through law school. My dad was horrified by the idea that his daughter wanted to be a lawyer. He'd wanted me to find a more feminine career, whatever that means."

"I have a hunch that if Aunt Letty had been born later, she would have made a name for herself in the business world. She had a sharp mind and a keen business sense. I understand she ran that ranch until Cole was old enough to take over."

"Well, that explains everything, doesn't it! Obviously Cade sees the resemblance between the two of us and feels right at home around me."

Matt laughed and stood. "You may have a point there," he said, going out the door. He paused in the doorway and added, "I have to admit that you're much better looking than she was . . . at least by the time I met her."

"Why, thank you, Mr. Callaway. You're very kind."

"Cade sure must enjoy a challenge," he said with a grin before disappearing down the hallway toward his office.

Candy stared at the empty doorway. So she was proud and stubborn, was she? Guess that meant that Callaways didn't have a corner on the market of those particular traits.

Chapter 10

The persistent ringing of the phone pulled Cade back from exhausted sleep. He hadn't gotten to bed until almost two o'clock. Even as he reached for the noisy instrument, he glanced at the clock beside the bed.

It was almost eight o'clock.

Damn, he'd overslept. This was probably Matt demanding to know where he was and when he intended to show up at the office.

The past few weeks had certainly taken their toll. Between his work in San Antonio and the demands made by the ranch, he felt as though he'd spent just as much time on the road as he had at either place.

He rolled over and grabbed the phone. "I'm comin', I'm comin'," he growled, already pulling himself up and shoving his hair out of his eyes.

"Obviously I've chosen an inopportune time to call, bro."

Cade's eyes opened wider, despite being red and swollen. "Clint! How the hell are you? And where are you? And when am I goin' to see you again?"

Clint laughed. "Lookin' in the mirror is the same as seeing me, good buddy. Despite that, I've missed you, too. I've been trying to track down Mom and Dad. Are they still in Europe?"

"Yeah, but I couldn't tell you where. I'm always getting these cheerful little postcards from Mom with no return address."

"I know. She keeps the postal workers busy, doesn't she?"

"So... where are you? Last I heard you were in Paris. You never seem to stay in D.C. much."

"At the moment I'm in Vegas, but this isn't work related."

"Finally took a vacation, did you?"

"Not exactly. I'm going to put in for one in the next few weeks, though, so that I can come see y'all. Actually I'm on what could be called a minihoneymoon."

"A what? Are you kidding me?"

"Nope. It was all a little sudden, I'll admit. More of a spur-of-the-moment type thing."

"My God, Clint. I can't believe it. The original loner is now married? What is this world coming to? Who is this paragon, and how did she ever manage to convince you to try marriage?"

"It was me convincing her. She's more adamant against being involved in a marriage than I am." He paused, as though gathering his thoughts. "Her name is Gabrielle Rousseau, or was until late last night. I've worked with her for several years, but we hadn't spent much time together until a few months ago when we worked an assignment together."

"You married another agent? This is unbelievable. I didn't even know you were allowed to do that."

"We're not too sure of the protocol, either. We may both be looking for jobs before much longer. You're the first person we've told about it. I called the folks first but the housekeeper said they were still away."

"Well, if I hadn't overslept, I'd have been away, as well."

"What's going on?" Cade filled Clint in on the lawsuit pending. When he had brought him up-to-date, Clint asked, "How long does Matt expect the case to run?"

"Oh, he thinks it will finish in a week. I certainly hope so. I've about run myself ragged. In fact, I'm hoping to take a couple of days' vacation, myself, once this is done."

"Not alone, I'm sure," Clint said with a hint of mockery.

"I'm being maligned, I swear I am. I've been on the straight and narrow for a long time now."

"What? A week? Two?"

"Make fun of me all you want, but if my memory serves me correctly, you owe me some money, don't you?"

"What are you talking about?"

"That bet we made in high school. We each predicted the other would be the first to marry. Obviously I said you'd get married before I would. Looks like I'm right."

Clint burst out laughing. "I should have known you'd remember that. My God, Cade. We made that bet almost twenty years ago."

"So? A bet is a bet. Pay up."

"What was it? I've forgotten."

"A hundred bucks."

"I suppose it could have been worse. The way you were always flirting with women, I felt safe betting practically anything you named back then."

"I like women, Clint. I don't necessarily flirt with them."

"Oh, yeah. Try explaining that to them, sometime."

"I've been trying to lately, but I guess my reputation is working against me."

"Oh-ho, could it be that my esteemed twin has met his match, so to speak?"

"I don't want to even talk about it for fear of putting a hex on the whole deal. Maybe by the time you get down here I'll have something to report."

"Good enough. I'll stay in touch and let you know when we're coming. I'm looking forward to your meeting Gabrielle, although I've already warned her about you. I explained that one of the reasons I suggested a fast wedding was to make darned sure you understood that this one is mine!"

"I've never poached on your turf and you know it."

"I couldn't afford to take the chance. Anyway, I'll talk to you soon."

Cade slowly hung up the phone, staring at it in wonder.

His brother had gotten married.

He was still having trouble adjusting to this new order of things. Somehow it seemed perfectly natural to be single, since both Clint and Matt were.

The phone rang again and he snatched it up. "H'lo?"

Matt's voice came on the line. "There you are. I thought you planned to be back here at the office this morning."

"I do. I just hung up the phone after talking to Clint. He ran off to Las Vegas and got married last night."

"No way. He must have been pulling your leg. Clint married? Now there's a joke."

"I don't think he was kidding, Matt. I've never heard that note in his voice before. He sounded relaxed and happy. It was amazing to talk to him."

"Hmmph. Better him than me is all I've got to say."

Cade had a sudden vision of Candy. "Yeah," he said absently. "I can't imagine being married to anybody." He knew it was a lie as soon as he said it. For a long time now he'd known that if he ever decided to settle down, it would be with someone like Candy. But Candy was one of a kind. He was very much afraid that if he didn't convince her that he would make a stable, dependable, true-blue husband, he might very well end up being single for the rest of his life.

The following Friday, Candy left the courthouse and returned to her office at about three o'clock. Matt and Cade had stayed to speak to the judge regarding the favorable judgment they'd received. All she wanted to do was to catch up on her mail and telephone messages, then go home and sleep for a week.

This had been a tough case, made tougher on her by the tension of having Cade in the office. She was embarrassed to realize that she'd actually missed that devil-may-care attitude of his during these long days at court. He was brisk, solemn and did an admirable job of testifying. The other side couldn't shake him.

She'd been proud of him. So had Matt. He'd told her that without Cade there, they wouldn't have had a prayer of winning this one. Only Cade had known the importance of some of the papers they'd had buried in boxes.

Candy knew she was experiencing the usual letdown that occurred after every trial. They'd been gearing up for this one for months. Both she and Matt had pushed other cases back to make more time for this one. Consequently her desk was piled high with matters she needed to handle.

But not today. She was going to look over a few things she'd left for her assistant to do, then call it a day.

She was immersed in her work some time later when she heard a brief tap on her open door. She looked up to see Cade standing there, grinning at her.

He still wore the dark suit he'd had on at trial. It made his black eyes look darker, if possible. There was one thing she could not deny... Cade Callaway was one good-looking man, even if he was fully aware of his effect on women.

"I'll tell you again," she said, leaning back in her chair and smiling at him, "You did us proud. I'm sure Matt's told you that we couldn't have won it without you."

He sauntered into the room in that loose-limbed walk of his and sat down across from her. "Thank you kindly, ma'am. That's the most positive remark I've ever heard you direct toward me."

"It's been a tough few weeks, hasn't it?" she replied, tossing her pen down and rolling her shoulders.

"Yes, ma'am, it has."

His polite tone and guileless gaze had her feeling ancient again. How did he manage to do that?

"You here to see Matt?"

"Nope. I'm here to collect on my bet." His voice remained gentle and very polite.

"Oh." The bet. Of course.

He slid down into his chair, extending his legs and crossing his ankles. "Would you say that we played by your rules and that I won fair and square?" He did not smile but continued to watch her with a look that she still didn't quite trust.

"I suppose," she said, with a slight shrug. "I will admit that you managed to surprise me, Mr. Callaway. You have been a perfect gentleman. I didn't think you had it in you." She pulled out the bottom drawer of her desk and picked up her purse. "How much do I owe you?"

With a grace that came natural to him, he stood and held out his hand. "We'll settle all of that later. In the meantime, we've got a plane to catch."

She stared at his hand as though it were a snake about to strike. "What in the world are you talking about?"

"All the arrangements have been made. We're flying to the Virgin Islands. That was the agreement, I believe."

She jumped to her feet. "Now wait just a minute here. The bet was for the loser to pay for the winner to go to a place of the winner's choice. It was not about—"

He held up his hand. "With the person of his or her choice. Remember? So...you're my choice. I'll run you by your place so you can pack a few things, unless you want to wait until we get down there to buy what you need."

No. This wasn't happening. How could he— How could she— What would Matt think if— *No.* It was impossible.

She tried to explain, but her words were almost as incoherent as her thoughts. "I can't. You must be crazy to think— I mean, I can't just take off like that. Look at this desk. I've got—"

"Forget your desk. It's Friday. You need a couple of days off. If we leave now, we'll get to the islands tonight, have all day tomorrow and most of Sunday there before we have to return."

She kept staring at him in disbelief. "You must be out of your mind."

"No, ma'am, I'm not. We made a bet, fair and square. We shook on it. Where I come from a person doesn't renege on a bet." He dropped his voice. "It's a little thing called integrity, I believe."

She could feel her temper starting to climb. "You think you're so smart, don't you? I should have known there was a trick to this." She attempted to mimic his deep voice saying, "'with the person of your choice—'" she finished in her own voice "—my aunt Sally!"

Without cracking a smile, Cade said, "I don't want to go to the islands with your aunt Sally, Candy. I chose you. So...are you going to honor our agreement?"

She slammed her desk drawer and slung her purse over her shoulder. "You think I won't go, don't you? You and Matt probably have me pegged as some silly, uptight old maid who's too afraid to—"

"Whoa . . . Slow down there, honey. I don't know what Matt has to do with any of this, but I sure as hell don't have you pegged as anybody but you. Besides, we both need a break. You don't think Matt's going to be sitting around the office all weekend, do you? We've all been under tremendous pressure these past few weeks. I, for one, know that I need a break and I can't think of anyone I'd rather spend a weekend with than you."

"Just what does that entail, spending the weekend?"

He laughed. Damn him, anyway. His eyes sparkled with good humor and she had a hunch she was the butt of the joke.

"Don't worry, Candy-cane, your virtue will remain intact as far as I'm concerned. We have separate rooms reserved. You'll be as safe as you want to be, I'll guarantee it."

"Fine. Let's go," she said, walking around the desk and pausing beside him. "Just don't think I'll ever be foolish enough to agree to another bet with you. I have definitely learned my lesson."

Chapter 11

"When you said 'reservations,' I thought you meant for our plane flight," Candy said to Cade, looking out the porthole of one of the Callaway Enterprises company jets. "You intend us to land in St. Thomas while I thought we were flying to Miami to make a connecting flight."

He smiled benignly. "You have to admit this is much more efficient."

"Since I'm the loser of this bet, how, exactly, do I pay for the flight?"

"You don't. The use of the plane is part of the fringe benefits of being a Callaway—we all have access to the toys we collect." He patted her hand consolingly. "But don't worry. I booked our rooms in your name."

"Gee, Cade, you're all heart," she grumbled.

"Thanks," he replied modestly. "I do try."

She leaned her head back and sighed. "I can certainly agree with that. You're one of the most trying men I have ever encountered in my life."

"Just one of my many charms," he agreed.

She shook her head, knowing that she would never have the last word with this man. She pulled out a small writing tablet from her purse in an effort to appear calm and collected. "So what's our agenda for our weekend?" she asked, just as though he were her secretary or tour guide.

He ignored her tone and genially answered her question. "We'll have an early night tonight since we've already had a full day. Then in the morning we'll do a little sight-seeing before roasting our bodies on the beach and cooling them in the water."

"The sun's not good for you" was all she could think of to say. Actually the trip seemed to have all the makings of her wildest fantasy come true. She had always wanted to see the Virgin Islands. She was still having trouble believing they were really on their way across the Gulf of Mexico.

Cade refused to let her grouchiness faze him. "I brought gallons of sun block, which I'm volunteering to rub all over your body, my sweet. Of course I expect the same kind of attention from you, as well."

She gave him a long, heavy stare, letting the silence speak for her. Eventually she said, "You know, Cade, I liked you much better when I didn't have to listen to the constant innuendos."

He grabbed his shirt right above his heart. "You like me? You actually like me? I'm not certain I can stand the shock. I've made much better strides these past few weeks than I ever dreamed I had."

She shook her head. He never let up, did he? Too tired to continue the verbal fencing, she closed her eyes, determined not to allow him to spoil her weekend.

She'd been telling the truth earlier. She was surprised to discover that she'd grown to like Cade since they'd been working so closely together. Perhaps it was time to admit to herself that she also enjoyed their verbal sparring. He had a quick mind that kept her on her toes. He was challenging and she'd always been a sucker for a challenge.

What she didn't want to do was to lose her heart to him. That way would lead to nothing but disaster. She was a career woman, after all. She didn't have time for the fast life that Cade seemed to revel in.

She must have fallen asleep because the next thing she knew, he was placing a tray over her lap. "Here you go. Can't have you starving to death before we even land."

She looked down at the fresh salad, the steaming bowl of soup and coffee. "Where did you get this?"

"We have all the comforts of home. I had it brought on earlier. All I needed to do was to heat the soup and make the coffee." He went back to the galley and returned with another tray just like hers. "I didn't figure we'd want anything too heavy...just something to tide us over."

"You're amazing, really," she said, unable to hide her amusement. "How does your brain keep track of all these details?"

"Oh, it just wants to keep busy, I guess. Hope you like broccoli-cheese soup."

"Don't be modest. Somehow you happened to find out that it's my favorite. You also managed to serve the salad with my favorite dressing."

"Glad to see I'm not losing any of my skills," he replied with a grin.

Once they'd eaten he insisted she rest while he took their trays back to the galley. She never heard him return. She slept until they were on their final approach to St. Thomas.

Cade found them transportation with a minimum amount of fuss. Candy was still yawning when they pulled up in front of the resort. "Wow," she muttered. "You really do it up big when you're spending other people's money."

"I'm sure you can afford it." He just grinned when she doubled her fist and hit him on the shoulder.

They each had brought a small bag, which Clint carried into the lobby of the hotel after paying the driver. She followed him, looking around with interest.

By the time she joined him at the desk, he was handing her a key. "Here you go. We're all checked in." Once again he picked up her bag along with his.

"I can carry that," she protested.

"You've got to be kidding. You're practically walking into doors and walls. I must say, you certainly sleep hard when you sleep. I'm surprised you woke up when you did."

"Surely you jest. We almost made a nosedive in order to land. Are you sure they allow jets to land on that runway? It seemed awfully short."

"We've got a good pilot."

He paused in front of two doors. He nodded to one. "That's your room. This one's mine." He opened his door with a key. When she just stood there, he paused and asked, "You want me to open it for you?"

"Don't bother. I have a hunch that if I were to go into your room with you I'd find a connecting door into mine."

"Have you always been so suspicious?"

"You bet I have. Ever since a young male cousin of mine wanted to play doctor when I was five years old and wanted me to be the patient instead of the nurse."

He took her key out of her hand and opened the door. "Go inside. If there is a connecting door, bolt it...put a chair against it...better yet...move the bed against it. Meanwhile, I'm going to get some sleep. I'm bushed."

With that he closed his door, leaving her standing there in the hallway.

All right, so she'd made a fool of herself. It certainly wasn't the first time and she had a hunch if she was around Cade much, it wouldn't be the last.

By morning she was in a much better frame of mind. For one thing, the room was comfortable. She did note the connecting door. However, the bolt was already in place. She'd left it that way once she'd made certain the outer door was secure. After that, she'd stripped off her clothes and fallen back into a deep sleep.

She eagerly got out of bed and hurried to the drapes, pulling them open and revealing a view she'd never believed could be real. Somehow, all the snapshots and professional photographs of the islands had seemed much too colorful not to be touched up in some darkroom.

Nature couldn't possibly have made the water so many beautiful shades of blue, nor the foliage so lush and green...and how did they get the sand so white?

All she could think about was jumping into her swimsuit and...the need for sunscreen. She'd brought what she had in her bathroom cabinet, but the container didn't have enough to cover her body in a two-piece suit.

She dug into her bag, pulled out the suit in question and put it on. She studied herself in the mirror with more than a little concern. She'd gained a little weight since she'd bought the thing last year. What had looked perfectly sedate then looked a little, uh, revealing to her now.

She walked over to the sliding glass door of her room, which lead to a small patio. Someone else was already enjoying the water this morning, she noted, watching as a well-built male surfaced from one of the waves and strode in knee-high water toward the beach. He looked as though he'd spent most of his life in the islands, considering his deep tan, his black hair glistening from the sun and water, his—

Oops. It was Cade whom she was standing there admiring with such appreciation.

It wasn't fair. It really wasn't. According to Matt, Clint and Cade were identical twins. Wasn't it enough that Cade was extraordinarily good-looking without the thought of two of them turned loose on an unsuspecting world?

Cade had mentioned last week that his brother had gotten married. If he was anything like Cade, he certainly wouldn't make a very tame spouse for any woman.

She watched Cade lean over and pick up a towel, his movements as coordinated as a ballet dancer. The brief swimsuit he wore—and she'd had to look twice to reassure herself that he was wearing one—was the same color as his tanned body.

She had a hunch he'd planned it that way.

So, what was she going to do? Hover here in the doorway and let him catch her eyeing him as if she were a hungry adolescent?

She spun on her heels and marched back into the bathroom where she grabbed a towel. Next, she picked up the tube of sun block, her sunglasses, slipped into her sandals and set out for the beach.

"Ah, glad to see you're up and moving this morning," he said, his bright smile in vivid contrast to his tanned face.

"It looks like you've already had some sun this morning, or are you always so dark?"

"It's my heritage, remember? My grandfather was Hispanic."

"Oh. I didn't know."

"I never knew him. His name was Antonio Alvarez. People called him Tony."

"Isn't that your oldest brother's name?"

"Yeah. His namesake. Our grandfather died while Mom was pregnant with my brother, so the only thing we have are pictures of him."

"How sad."

"None of us grew up with grandparents. Aunt Letty was the only one of that generation we knew."

"Matt was telling me about her one time."

His grin flashed again. "She was a pistol. She used to fuss at us all the time about getting so dark in the sun and looking like little heathens, as she called us. We tan quickly and it fades slowly." He took his time looking her over. "You, on the other hand, are going to need all the help you can get not to turn a nice, bright red before the day is over. I've never seen such pale skin."

"I know. I have to be very careful or I'm in trouble before I realize it."

He took the tube of cream from her and looked at it. "There's not much here."

She gave him her sweetest smile. "That's because I wasn't given time to buy more. This is left over from last season."

He was already unscrewing the cap. "Turn around."

Although she didn't necessarily approve of his tone, she was amenable to his actions. She turned around before making a face. She almost flinched when he put his hand on her neck and began to rub across her shoulders. He worked quickly and efficiently down her back. When he touched her thigh she quickly stepped away. "I can do the rest," she said.

"Not until I get some more cream. I'll be right back." He moved toward his room in the easy lope of a trained athlete. She turned and deliberately looked out to sea, admiring the view and reminding herself of all her lofty ideals about not getting involved with this man.

She'd have to be a robot not to succumb to the exotic atmosphere of the island. It was a veritable paradise. It would be all too easy to pretend for a couple of days that she and Cade were the only two people in the world, with no history between them, with no wide difference in life-styles and dreams.

She wouldn't put it past Cade to have planned this entire trip as her seduction. He was used to getting whatever woman he wanted, no doubt. She just had to keep reminding herself that she didn't have to be one of them.

Chapter 12

By dinner that night she could no longer remember why it would be such a bad thing to wrap herself around Cade as if she were a vine.

He'd been utterly charming all day. From the way he acted, a person would think that he had lost the bet, he was so determined that she be comfortable at all times.

Now that they were halfway through dinner he was suggesting they dance once the meal was over. The band was good, the music subtly wrapping around those within hearing in an alluring way.

She was tired of fighting the seductiveness of it all.

"I'd love to dance," she said, knowing that she was tossing her common sense away. She no longer cared.

Of course he was a smooth dancer, she reminded herself sometime later. He'd had plenty of practice. He's an absolute master at setting and keeping a mood. She certainly knew that by now.

The music was slow jazz, and he moved to it as though born with music inside his soul. She closed her eyes and leaned her head against his chest, savoring the feel of his body pressed against hers. How could one man feel this good?

"Candy?"

"Mmm."

"I think the band has decided to call it a night," he said, sounding amused. Only then did she realize that she was still plastered against him and there was no more music. Other couples were drifting from the floor.

She immediately stepped back from him.

"How about a walk on the beach? The moon's more than half-full. It should give off plenty of light."

Of course. There were no half measures in Cade's arsenal.

They stopped by her room so that she could slip on a pair of sandals, then went out to the beach. They weren't the only couple on the beach, which she found reassuring. It really was a beautiful night, and the scent of exotic flowers wafting on the breeze gave her an excuse to take a deep breath, and remind herself that she was a mature woman with a mind of her own and that none of this had to affect her in the least, not unless she allowed it to do so.

Cade took her hand. She didn't pull away.

"You know, I've known you for the past two years, but don't really know much about you. Are you from San Antonio originally?"

"No. I was born in east Texas," she replied, watching the way the moonlight touched the waves, making them sparkle. "My dad was an oil field worker. He was killed on one of the sites when I was twenty-two."

"I'm sorry to hear that. Family is important. Are you an only child?"

"My brother is two years younger than me. Mother kept us going, together with the money she received from Dad's accident. I'd already applied for law school and she insisted that I continue with my plans."

"Do you see your family often?"

"My brother travels a great deal. He's based in Houston but flies all over the world. Mom's retired and now lives near Ted so she can see the grandchildren. She dotes on them, and gets along well with my sister-in-law."

Dear Reader,

YOU MAY BE A MAILBOX AWAY FROM BEING OUR NEW MILLION $$ WINNER!

Scratch off the gold on Game Cards 1-7 to automatically qualify for a chance to win a cash prize of up to $1 Million in lifetime cash! Do the same on Game Cards 8 & 9 to automatically get free books and a free surprise gift -- and to try Silhouette's no-risk Reader Service. It's a delightful way to get our best novels each month -- at discount -- with no obligation to buy, ever. Here's how it works, satisfaction fully guaranteed:

After receiving your free books, if you don't want any more, just write "cancel" on the accompanying statement, and return it to us. If you do not cancel, each month we'll send you 6 additional novels to read and enjoy & bill you just $3.24 each plus 25¢ delivery and applicable sales tax, if any.* That's the complete price, and -- compared to cover prices of $3.99 each -- quite a bargain!

You may cancel at any time, but if you choose to continue, every month we'll send you 6 more books, which you may either purchase at the discount price...or return to us and cancel your subscription.

P.S. Don't Forget to include your Bonus Token.

SEE BACK OF BOOK FOR SWEEPSTAKES DETAILS. ENTER TODAY, AND... *Good Luck!*

"Does she ever urge you to produce more grand-children for her?"

Candy chuckled. "Oh, no. She knew by the time I left for college that I would never be happy in a domestic role."

"You mean you don't want a family?"

"I'm not qualified to raise one. I've never had the slightest inclination to learn how to run a household or take care of babies."

"A died-in-the-wool professional person."

"That's right."

"That doesn't mean you couldn't have a hus-band, does it?"

"Why, are you applying for the position?"

He burst out laughing. "Nothing shy about you, is there?"

"I'm just trying to understand the reason for your line of questioning, that's all. How could my atti-tude toward marriage be of any interest to you?"

"Maybe I'm taking a survey among the single people I know."

She thought about the recent news of his broth-er's marriage. It was quite possible that Cade had been a little shaken by the news. "I see," she drawled. "Then let's turn it around. Why aren't you married and when do you intend to provide grand-children for your parents?"

Cade laughed. "I don't mind answering. I fully expect to settle down with one woman someday. Just not anytime soon. And as far as grandchildren, the folks already have five. Tony has three and Katie has two. That gives them plenty to spoil.''

''Do you see yourself as a father?''

''Haven't given it much thought, to be honest. If you mean do I go all soft and mushy inside whenever I'm around a baby, the answer is no.''

''Somehow I can't really picture you as the soft and mushy type.''

''If my wife really wanted a family, I'd consider it. I believe it takes two committed parents to provide a decent upbringing for a child.''

''At least we agree on that.''

''Oh, I think we agree on many things, Candycane.''

''I was hoping that you would forget about that disgusting nickname you made up.''

He stopped and turned toward her. The breeze ruffled his hair so that it fell across his forehead. Still holding her hand, he tugged her closer, then wrapped his arms around her. ''The thing is, Candy,'' he whispered, his lips brushing her ear, ''whenever I'm around you I get this really strong urge to lick you all over. I bet you taste as sweet as your name.'' He followed up his outrageous statement by grasping her lobe between his teeth and nibbling, then running his tongue over it soothingly.

Shivers ran all the way down to her toes. She attempted to pull away at the same time she opened her mouth to protest. Once again he took advantage of the situation by kissing her, claiming a possession he didn't deserve and she hadn't intended to give him.

With the first probing stab of his tongue she forgot what she'd intended to say to him, forgot his high-handed ways, forgot everything but the sensations he was evoking from deep inside her.

He had awakened a sleeping tiger within her, one she'd never known existed and would have vehemently denied had anyone suggested that it resided there. She'd been teased and tantalized for the past twenty-four hours by this man and by damn, she was tired of it!

With a strength she'd never before tested, she wrapped her arms around him and kissed him back with feverish intensity. When he tried to pause for breath, she tightened her hold, unwilling to lose touch with all these wondrous feelings exploding within her.

He groaned, as though losing whatever grip he had on his own self-control. He picked her up and strode into the deeper shadows beneath the trees, his mouth still devouring hers. By the time he lowered her to her feet once more, they were both breathing hard. He jerked off his jacket and tossed it on the grass, then slowly lowered her onto the jacket while coming down on top of her.

Candy no longer cared where they were. She wanted this man with a fierceness that had never been drawn out of her by anyone before. She pushed away the offending clothing that kept her from touching him, from exploring all the wonderful curves and smooth hardness that made him who he was.

Almost frantic with need, she lifted herself to him and he moved deep within her, claiming her as his, pushed beyond all restraints to experience the woman who had haunted him for years.

Their coming together was too explosive to last. With a cry of frustration and acknowledgment of his complete loss of control, Cade surged against her, relieved to feel her contractions tighten around him, hearing her cry of release deep in her throat.

They lay there in the grass, arms wrapped around each other, fighting for breath. Her skirt was shoved high on her hips. He still wore his pants, although open, and his shirt, also open.

Cade raised his head as reality slowly returned, and looked around. They were hidden in midnight shadows, the gleam of white sand several feet away. The moon highlighted the foam as the waves slipped across the shoreline.

At least he lay over her so that neither one of them was exposed should someone happen to walk by.

Oh, God, what had he done? This wasn't what he'd intended to have happen. Well, actually, it was exactly what he'd hoped would happen...sometime...maybe later when he'd convinced her he wasn't some Lothario who got his kicks from deceiving and seducing beautiful women. He'd meant to take it slow, to allow her time to get to know him, to trust him.

Trust him? That was a laugh now. He wouldn't be surprised if she never spoke to him again.

He glanced down at her, still carefully keeping most of his weight off her. She lay beneath him, and from the meager amount of light available he couldn't see her expression, only that her eyes were closed.

He started to move and she tightened her hold on him. "Don't go," she whispered. "Not yet."

That was the most encouraging thing she'd ever said to him. "You must be uncomfortable."

"No" was all she said, her fingers underneath his shirt caressing his spine in a lazy movement.

After another prolonged silence, he spoke again.

"Why don't we go back to our rooms where we'd be more comfortable?" he suggested gruffly.

"You're certainly concerned about my comfort." He could hear the amusement in her voice.

"Yes, I am," he replied quite honestly.

She allowed her hands to slide around to his chest, touching him lightly. "All right," she said with a sigh. "If you insist."

He moved and straightened his clothing, then helped her to her feet. Without saying a word, he picked up his jacket and draped it over his shoulder before grasping her hand and leading her back to the beach. They walked along the shore in silence, taking their time. When they approached their rooms, he started to let go of her hand, but she held his firmly, leading him into her room.

She didn't turn on a light. The moonlight gave them enough light to see each other's faces. She took his jacket and carefully laid it on a chair, then slid his shirt off as well. When she unfastened his pants and let them fall to his ankles, Cade knew that she was being much more generous than he deserved.

Not only had he not turned her off to lovemaking completely, but she was obviously willing to discover more about it.

He unfastened her dress and allowed it to slither down her body, lying in a pool at her feet. She was beautiful standing there in the light and he wanted her with an intensity he'd never felt for anyone, ever, despite the fact that he'd just made love to her.

This time, however, he intended to take his time and explore every inch of this luscious lady, even if it took him the rest of the night. As a matter of fact, he was counting on it.

He quickly disposed of her filmy underwear and lowered her to the bed. Leaning over her, he cupped her breasts with his hands and nuzzled them, stroking them with his thumb and tongue, causing her to squirm and sigh.

Still taking his time, he began to follow an invisible trail along her body, placing kisses over her abdomen, down her thigh and calf, reversing the direction on her other leg.

By the time he reached her waist once again, she was quivering.

He'd been affected as well. Cade forgot all about his planned seduction when she reached for him and guided him to her once more. He sank into her with a sigh of relief.

Cade knew he never wanted to leave her.

Chapter 13

Candy was dreaming a most luscious dream. She didn't want it to end. The warmth of the sun soothed her skin while masculine fingers stroked across her breasts, causing them to draw up into sensitive buds of pleasure.

She shifted slightly, her thigh brushing against the hard, rounded surface of—

Her eyes flew open, suddenly aware that this wasn't a dream.

"Good morning," a deep voice growled in her ear.

She blinked, turning her head on the pillow and staring into a pair of dark, sleepy eyes.

"Cade?" she squeaked.

"Who else did you expect to find in your bed this morning?"

Oh, dear Lord, what had she done? She'd really blown it this time. Where was all that willpower and self-discipline she'd always taken so much pride in when she needed it?

Obviously those were the very items she'd neglected to pack for this impromptu trip to paradise. Lordy, Lordy, what was she going to do now?

"Did you sleep well?" he asked, coming up on his elbow. His other hand continued to stroke and massage her breasts while his knee somehow became insinuated between her thighs.

"I, uh, very well, thank you very much," she absently replied, her mind frantically searching for a way out of this situation.

"So polite," he murmured, trailing kisses from her ear, down her neck and along her collarbone.

She could feel all of her bones melting like caramel candy left out in the sun. "I, uh, don't think we should—oh!—I mean, don't you think we should, mmmm— Oh, Cade, I—"

"I love to hear you say my name in that tone of voice. You have no idea how often I've fantasized about your speaking to me in just that way."

Before she guessed what he was going to do, Cade shifted so that he was between her legs, his arousal pressing urgently against her. He lowered his mouth to her breast and began to tease her nipple with his tongue.

She groaned, her fingers suddenly spiking through his hair. She couldn't believe what was happening to her. She'd lost all sense of propriety. How could she possibly be—

And then she forgot all the lectures. She forgot everything...but what Cade was doing to her that set her body quivering and her emotions reeling.

"This doesn't change things between us," Candy said to Cade over a belated brunch served on the terrace of the hotel's restaurant. They had a clear view of the beach while shaded by an oversize umbrella that covered their table.

He almost choked on his coffee. Hastily Cade put his cup down. "What the hell is that supposed to mean?"

"What part of it don't you understand?"

"It sure as hell does change things between us. We've just spent the most erotic, passionate weekend of my life together. How can you possibly say that—"

"Nonsense. You probably do this type of thing all the time, Cade. It has your signature stamped all over it. What could be more seductive than to whisk a woman away to a tropical paradise? And what's even better, she gets to pay for it. Sounds exactly like something you would do." She took a sip of her orange juice before fluttering her lashes at him in a pseudocoy look and adding, "Not that I'm complaining, you understand. It was worth every single penny it's costing me, sweetie. I'll be more than happy to see that you are highly recommended to whomever you wish."

"Will you stop that? You don't fool me a bit. All right. So this was all new to you. Don't you think I know that? I wanted your first time to be special. Of course I didn't exactly intend it to take place on the beach, but honey, you and I are like oil and fire together. Talk about spontaneous combustion! I always knew that if you'd just give us a chance that we could—"

"You're embarrassing me, Cade. You might be used to chatting about your love life, but I'd prefer another topic of conversation. All I'm saying is, nothing important has really changed for us. I work in the family law firm. I'll do my best to tolerate your innuendos whenever you pop into the office—now that I can better understand some of them!—and we'll each get on with our life. This weekend was the most daring thing I've ever done in my life. I still can't quite believe this is me, sitting here." She looked around at the other tables and people sitting there. "If I ever feel the need for another escape weekend, I certainly know where I'll want to come."

"And with whom?" he asked in a silky voice.

She met his gaze with a limpid smile. "Oh, you've been an excellent instructor, Cade, but I think I can handle everything on my own from here."

"Damn it, Candy, you've carried your little joke far enough. Just cut it out, okay? So maybe I have gone a little overboard in the past, trying to get you to acknowledge my existence. Maybe I came on a little strong, okay?"

"A little?"

"All right. A lot. But do you have any idea how I feel about you? I've been relentlessly pursuing you for two years."

"Of course you have...between escorting every good-looking blonde in the state to the many social functions around, poor darling. I can only imagine how difficult life has been for you these past couple of years."

He flushed. "Well, what did you expect me to do? As I recall, there were many of those functions where I invited you to attend with me and you turned me down," he said through clinched teeth.

"Yes, for some odd reason I didn't feel that I wanted to get involved with someone as irresponsible as you are. I believe this weekend is certainly a case in point."

"What in the hell are you talking about? What was irresponsible about a couple days off after the schedule we've both been keeping?"

"Perhaps you have a point, except that you knew how you wanted this weekend to end and I was just dumb enough, and naive to the extreme, to think I could hang on to my self-control."

"Wow, you've lost me here. What, exactly, are you talking about?"

He honestly didn't know, she could see that by his puzzled expression. What better example did she need of his cavalier attitude toward women and responsibility than the quizzical look on his face?

"Birth control," she replied tersely.

His face remained blank for a few seconds, then his face flushed. He looked as though he'd never heard of the idea before, which didn't surprise her in the least.

It was a matter of pride to her that he not know how shaken she was when she'd first realized that neither of them had discussed the need for protection.

It was only after he'd returned to his room that morning to dress and she'd finally been alone—after they'd ended up showering together and making love again!—that it finally dawned on her she'd never given the idea of protection a thought during the past twelve hours.

She had certainly been living a fantasy. She'd been so wrapped up in all the new things she was experiencing that she'd forgotten a lifetime of caution.

No wonder they called him the Texas Stud!

She knew she wasn't being fair to place the sole blame on him. She had been just as guilty as he, of course. However, he'd already admitted that he knew she wasn't used to this sort of thing. He could have asked. Or better yet, he could have come prepared.

Cade continued to meet her gaze, despite his ruddy cheeks. His devastating smile was gone. She couldn't remember ever having seen him so serious.

"Is there a chance you may be pregnant?" he finally asked in a low voice.

Hanging on to her pride for all she was worth, she said, "I would think it a possibility, given the past few hours' activities. There's no way to know at the moment, of course."

Cade could feel the dismay seep through him. Not at the possibility of her becoming pregnant . . . never that . . . but at her attitude toward him since they'd sat down to a late breakfast.

All her walls were up once again, her armor in place, her cold attitude toward him totally dismissing the joy they had shared.

Of course he shouldn't have been so surprised. Isn't that what he'd expected when they'd left the beach last night? Hadn't he been more surprised at her fiery response to him?

He hadn't realized how much her loving warmth had given him hope that he'd finally broken through the brittle veneer with which she surrounded herself. The knowledge that he'd been wrong wrung his heart.

He'd been so close to winning her, or so he thought.

Cade finally spoke, breaking the silence that had stretched between them. "I hope you are."

She looked as shocked as if he'd slapped her. "What did you say?" she finally whispered.

He leaned forward, his tone brusque. "You heard me. I hope to God that you are pregnant. It will be the only edge I'll ever have with you. If you're pregnant, we'll get married. We'll—"

She was already shaking her head. "Absolutely not. There is no way I would marry you, Cade. Maybe you don't understand the reputation you have for playing the field, of never getting serious about anyone, of dodging commitments. Why, just yesterday you said that you didn't intend to marry for years and years, that you were not ready to settle down." She shook her head. "The idea of you playing the role of a husband and a father is more than my imagination can possibly grasp."

He leaned back in his chair and crossed his arms over his chest. "I don't care what you've heard about me or what you think you know about me. I am not promiscuous. A person would have to be crazy to bed-hop in this day and age. Besides, no man could possibly live up to the kind of reputation that's been attached to my name. I've never cared what they said about me before. But I do now, if that's what you're basing your judgments on. Think about it. During the past two years that you've worked with my family, you've seen how everything about our family gets exaggerated. Why wouldn't my reputation, as well?''

She eyed him, warily, but he could see that he had her attention and that he was at least making her look at some of her assumptions about him. It was time to lighten the tension a little.

He gave her a lopsided smile. ''The thing is, Candy, darlin', if all I'd wanted from you was some fast weekend fling, then this is the time I'd be backpedaling about my feelings for you, instead of letting you know how I feel.''

Candy looked away from the intent expression in his eyes. She was way out of her depths here and she knew it. It wasn't just what had happened between them physically. She hadn't really expected to remain a virgin for the rest of her life.

No. It was what he had made her feel when they'd been together . . . as though she was the most fascinating woman he'd known, as though he appreciated her for who and what she was as well as delighted in making love to her.

Her smile was a little forced. ''Don't worry, Cade. I'm not going to hold you to anything you might have said while in the throes of passion.''

He frowned. ''Throes of passion. What the hell is that?''

Still trying for a light touch, she said, "Oh, something I once read." She chuckled. "Actually it sounds a little uncomfortable, don't you think?"

He glanced around them, then said, "Let's take another walk on the beach. It's broad daylight, so you don't have to worry about my dragging you into the underbrush." He stood and held out his hand.

What he didn't understand was that she knew she'd been the one to instigate their lovemaking last night. She'd been the one who brought him to her room. Cade was not the one she didn't trust; it was herself.

However, it was a beautiful day and they would be leaving in a matter of hours. She might as well enjoy as much of it as she could.

She allowed him to pull her to her feet and lead her through the tables until they reached the steps that led down to the sand.

"It is a beautiful day, don't you think?" she said when he didn't say anything. He'd dropped her hand as soon as they reached the beach. She'd stuck both her hands into the pockets of her sundress.

He looked around as though he'd just noticed the blue sky, the bluer water and the white sands. "Did you remember to put on some sunscreen?"

"Yes."

"Good." Then he lapsed into silence once again.

She was glad she'd bought the wide-brimmed sun hat the day before. It kept the heat from beating down on her head. Cade appeared oblivious to the sun, but then he'd worked out in it most of his life.

The beach curved around, and in the distance the smooth sand was broken by a promontory. When they got to it, she looked at Cade to see if he wanted to turn around or to pause in the shade of the trees.

He didn't appear to be aware of where they were, he was so lost in thought.

Now here was a side to the man that she'd never seen before he'd come to San Antonio to work on the case. When he wasn't busy dispensing his easy charm, he appeared older, harder and just a little intimidating.

What did it matter, after all? Once this weekend was over, her bet paid off, she'd have no more reason to see or speak to him. Her life was the city, while his was the ranch.

He surprised her when he started speaking, but it was what he was saying that stunned her into speechlessness.

"All right, Candy. Here it is," he said, turning to her and taking her hands in his. "I am willing to make a commitment to you, starting here and now. I will not see or date another woman. We will start spending time together. We will get to know each other better. We will find out if we're compatible. We'll—"

Was this what he'd been mulling over ever since they'd been on the beach? He made it sound as though she had some hold over him and he was forced to negotiate with her. What nonsense. He owed her nothing and she needed to make that immediately clear.

"What if I want to date other men?" she asked, pleased with how reasonable she sounded.

He, on the other hand, sounded anything but reasonable. "Hell, no, you aren't going to date other men! A commitment's a commitment."

"What I'm saying to you, Cade," she said very patiently, "is that I'm not ready to make a commitment... to you or to anyone. Heavens, I've just discovered a side of myself that I never knew existed." She sighed—trying hard not to show her amusement at how he was beginning to bristle—and said as jauntily as possible, given how her knees were shaking. "I had no idea sex could be so awesome, so consuming, so deliciously decadent. There's a whole new world out there for me to explore!" She couldn't look at him or he'd immediately recognize that she was teasing the heck out of him.

His face looked like a thundercloud. "My God, I've created a monster."

She turned away and studiously focused on the horizon, her lips quivering with laughter. Mr. Callaway didn't seem to like being on the other end of teasing. What a heady sense of power it gave her to know that she could have such an effect on him.

Was that why he enjoyed teasing her so much?

Now, *there* was a thought to ponder.

Cade stared at her slender back in frustration. He'd never been in a situation like this in his life. Hell, he'd never felt this way about a woman before in his life. He had no idea how to deal with her attitude toward him.

"You know," she said without turning around. "I'd really like to go swimming once more before we have to pack." She turned toward him, her eyes bright. "How about it?"

Bemused by the contented look on her face, Cade nodded slowly. This woman was going to drive him insane, he could tell. Unfortunately it was too late for him to walk away. Much, much too late.

Chapter 14

"Good morning, Matt," Candy said as she passed him in the hall early the following Monday morning.

Carrying a cup of coffee, he absently responded, "Mornin'. Have a good weekend?"

She froze in her stride and spun around while he continued toward his office. "What do you mean by that?"

He stopped as though she'd shot him between the shoulder blades. Slowly Matt turned and stared at her, really seeing her for the first time. What he saw seemed to amuse him.

"Nothing in particular, why do you ask?" he replied with a smile.

"I thought— I mean—" Candy suddenly saw the yawning chasm before her.

"It's obvious you must have had a nice weekend, from the looks of things. You're tanned, so you must have gotten some sun."

"Uh, yes. Yes, I did."

"Good. You needed a break after the hours we've been putting in lately." He turned away and continued down the hallway.

She couldn't let him walk away. "I'm sorry for being so touchy, Matt. You've greeted me with the same question every Monday since I've worked here. Don't know why I overreacted."

He paused at the door to his office and grinned at her. "I could guess, but I'm not going to. It's past time you developed a social life. It's also none of my business and I certainly wasn't trying to pry."

"I know." She smiled at him. "You've been a very good friend as well as partner. I wouldn't want to offend you."

"Don't worry about it, okay?" he said, stepping inside his office and closing the door.

Good grief! she thought as she walked into her office. She was being as jumpy as a schoolboy in the principal's office. Matt had been right. It was nobody's business how she'd spent her weekend or with whom.

She sat down behind her desk and pulled a stack of files in front of her. With forced concentration she went to work on the backlog of cases that awaited her.

Candy could hear her phone ringing before she unlocked her apartment door that evening. She'd worked until after seven, then had gone to the grocery store. She was tired, not only from the day she'd just put in, but because she hadn't slept all that well the night before.

Juggling the bags of groceries with her purse and keys, she fumbled to open the door. It was probably her mother calling. Candy hadn't spoken to her in a couple of weeks.

She grabbed the phone and, sounding a little breathless answered. "H'lo?"

"Candy? Is that you?"

He might not recognize her voice, but she had no trouble identifying her caller. "Hello, Cade."

"I wasn't sure if I had the right number. I've called several times this evening and just let it ring. Don't you have an answering machine?"

She put the groceries on the kitchen counter and sat on one of her bar stools before answering him. "No. I don't get that many calls at home, usually just my family. They know they can reach me at the office if they don't find me here."

"Oh. Somehow I had the impression that you wouldn't want me calling you at the office."

"I said my family, Cade."

"Yeah. I know." He sounded rather subdued, for Cade. "I won't keep you. I was just wondering if you'd like to come out to the ranch next weekend? You've never seen it, have you?"

She didn't answer right away. In truth, she wasn't certain what she could say. Wanting to go to the ranch wasn't the issue. Whether it was wise for her to spend any more time around Cade Callaway was the real question—and her heart and intellect were tugging her in opposite directions.

"No, I've never seen it," she finally answered, dodging the first question.

"Well, I was thinking that I could pick you up after work on Friday. It's only a couple of hours back to the ranch. Then Saturday I could take you out, either in the Jeep or on horseback, whichever you prefer, and show you some of the prettier parts of the place."

"I, uh, don't think—" She closed her eyes, trying to keep her traitorous heart from betraying how glad she was that he had called her. She took a deep breath and exhaled slowly in an attempt to calm her breathing. "Why don't I drive out Saturday morning, instead?" she finally replied. "You could give me directions, couldn't you?"

"Sure." The bounce was back in his voice. "That would be great. How soon could you make it?"

"I have my usual weekend chores to do, which didn't get done this past weekend, as you know. I really need to take care of those. If I left here at noon, we'd still have most of the afternoon, wouldn't we?''

"True. Plus, we'd have most of Sunday before you'd need to return to the city."

"All right, Cade. I just got home with groceries that need to be put away, okay? I'll see you on Saturday."

"Yeah, see you."

Cade hung up the phone, feeling as though he'd just won a vital concession from Candy. He'd been calling her apartment since around six o'clock. His imagination had played all kinds of games with him when she hadn't answered. He'd been relieved to know that her absence had been due to a trip to the grocery store, and not because she was seeing someone else.

His most positive imaginings couldn't have delivered a more perfect weekend than the one just past. Somehow his guardian angel must have been looking out for him.

If there was such a thing as a guardian angel.

The hours had flown by yesterday. They'd played in the water and once again Candy had surprised him with a new aspect of her character. He'd seen the competent attorney, the aloof woman, and the woman who ignited his passions as well as her own. For the rest of the day he'd gotten to know a playful, teasing woman whom he'd found delightful.

She'd managed to keep him off center the entire time they'd spent together.

At one point he'd taken as much teasing as he could handle. He'd grabbed her when she surfaced beside him in the sparkling water and kissed her, claiming her in the only way he knew how.

Her response was everything he could have wanted it to be. He knew, then, that this particular woman among all the ones he'd known had completely stolen his heart.

Now all he needed to do was to convince her of that.

"If I do have a guardian angel," he muttered to himself, "now's the time to help me convince Candy that we could make a go of a relationship." He didn't know how—with him living on the ranch and her living in the city, or when—since she was determined to keep her guard up whenever he was around, but he definitely knew why.

Cade Callaway was in love for the first time in his life and all his previous beliefs about commitment, marriage and a family had flown out the window.

What if she *was* pregnant? The thought made his toes curl with longing. It was true that Clint married first, but maybe it wasn't too late to beat his competitive brother at something.

Cade went upstairs to his bedroom, whistling.

Candy did everything she could think of during that week to return her life to the way it had been before her weekend with Cade. She chatted with her mother, inquired about her brother and his family, went to her aerobics class, had her hair trimmed, caught up on her work at the office, went to a movie with a friend... but none of her activities stopped her thoughts once she went to bed at night.

She relived each and every thing she and Cade had done together—their time on the beach, the moonlight strolls and the hours of lovemaking they had shared. She still had trouble recognizing the person she'd been with him—passionate, abandoned, eager to experience everything that Cade could teach her about loving someone.

How could she pretend that none of that had happened? How could she see him again without remembering how his mouth felt against her body, remembering the scent and taste of him?

And yet she'd agreed to drive to the ranch on Saturday.

The truth was that she had always been intrigued by the man and his reputation. How could she explain having read every article she could find about him? His teasing comments had frightened her because they came so easily for him. She still didn't trust his sincerity.

Oh, she believed that he had enjoyed himself with her. It would have been difficult for him to fake his reaction to her, but he had mentioned a commitment, something she was sure he'd never experienced.

No. She couldn't take a chance on being hurt. She couldn't undo what had happened between them. He had taught her so much about herself that it was almost frightening. Now she knew how vulnerable she was. She would just have to make certain she wasn't alone with him in an intimate situation again.

She refused to think about the possibility of being pregnant. If that came to pass, she would just have to deal with it. She certainly wouldn't look to Cade for any assistance. She couldn't imagine anything worse than having him marry her out of a sense of obligation.

Ariel was worried, really worried. She knew that Cade and Candy were going to be having a baby boy in approximately nine months. It was part of the plan. She'd been pleased that Cade had so quickly understood that Candy was the mate he'd been looking for.

Candy's reticence had been understandable, given the reputation Cade had so negligently allowed to become a part of his life.

Ariel felt that Cade would overcome Candy's doubts, given time. However, their impetuous behavior had moved everything about their courtship onto a fast track.

It was up to Ariel to make certain that Cade proposed marriage before either of them knew that she was pregnant. Given the way Cade was feeling, it wouldn't take much more than a nudge for him to declare himself.

Ariel decided it was up to her to provide that nudge.

Chapter 15

"Are you sure you're up to riding much farther?" Cade asked Candy Saturday afternoon. She'd chosen to go horseback riding and they'd been out for about an hour.

She smiled at his obvious concern. "I think I'm okay, Cade. You don't have to worry. I'm fairly active despite my desk job."

"It's just that riding uses a different set of muscles than 'most anything else you do."

"Why don't we ride down to that clump of trees? It looks like there's water there."

"Yes. Some member of the family built a spillway over the creek years ago so that we could swim." His eyes lit up. "Maybe you'd like to swim."

"Another day, perhaps. I didn't bring my suit."

"Don't tell me you're going to be modest with me now! Remember me? I'm the guy you showered with just a week ago."

She took her time looking him up and down. "Really? I thought you looked a little familiar. I probably didn't recognize you with your clothes on."

"Very funny."

"I'm not really in a swimming mood. As nice as the creek could be, nothing could possibly compare to swimming in the lagoon...all that warm water and hot sun." She laughed. "Who knows? I may never swim anywhere else again!"

He nudged his horse to take the lead and they started toward the river. "I have to admit I've never seen anything quite like it, myself. I'm glad you chose the islands to visit."

"Which reminds me, you were less than honest with me, Cade."

He glanced at her. "Oh, yeah? Now what sin have I committed?"

"You paid the hotel bill."

"Oh, that. Well, I'd made the reservations in your name, but of course I gave them my credit card, so it was only natural that I pay."

"But when it came time to check out, you sent me off on a silly errand so that—"

"Buying souvenirs isn't silly. It was more efficient to get the bill settled while you shopped, that's all."

"But you won the bet."

He gave her a very wolfish grin. "And I was justly rewarded. It will be a weekend I'll never forget."

They reached the shade of the trees and he dismounted, leading their horses to the water, then helping her out of the saddle. She took a couple of steps, then winced.

"What did I tell you?"

"I can't believe I'm already tender," she said ruefully, rubbing her rear. "Guess I'm not in as good a shape as I thought."

He took her hand and led her to a grassy area. "We'll rest here for a while. If you don't feel like riding back, I'll go get the Jeep." He sat down beside her and leaned back, resting on his elbows.

She shook her head, then carefully lowered her body until she was stretched out beside him. "Thanks, but I don't think that will be necessary," she said. "I'll be fine. But next time, I'll listen when you suggest I use caution."

"Now you tell me! Of course if I wanted you to use caution around me, I wouldn't be plotting ways to get you alone every weekend."

"You mean bringing me out here was part of a plan?" She looked up into the trees that were providing them shade, feeling at peace with her world.

He rolled onto his side so that he was facing her. "I wanted you to see how I live."

She thought of the sprawling stucco and red-tiled hacienda he called the Big House. He had given her a tour of the place once she'd arrived at the ranch. She'd had no idea the ranch was so large. When she'd seen the cluster of buildings at the bottom of one of the hills once she'd turned off the highway, she thought it was a small town. It was only when she got closer that she discovered all the buildings were part of the ranch operation.

She turned her head so that her gaze met his. "Do you live here alone?"

He laughed. "Hardly. There must be fifty people working around this place."

"I mean, are there other family members who live here?"

"They come and go. My uncle Cody raised his family here but they've all scattered, bought their own places. He and Carina live here when they aren't traveling. Why do you ask?"

"I wondered if you ever get lonely so far from the city."

"No. I enjoy a social life, but I can't say I prefer it. Ranching is in my blood. I could never do anything else."

"I see."

Silence grew between them. Cade was content with the lack of conversation. He wanted Candy to understand who he was and why the ranch was so important to him. He knew he loved and wanted her, but he also knew he couldn't change his life-style to make her happy. She would have to accept him as he was, and he already knew how difficult a job he had ahead of him in order to overcome her prejudices toward him.

Her visit today was encouraging. However, he wasn't going to rush her. They had years ahead of them, so there was no reason that he could see to get into a hurry now that things were going so well.

"No, I am not going to share a room with you tonight," Candy said without hesitation.

Cade grinned. "Can't blame me for asking, now can you?"

They were seated in the den, sipping coffee after dinner when Cade made the suggestion that they share one of the master suites in the house.

"That is not why I came out here for the weekend."

"All right."

"I've always been curious about the place, that's all."

"I understand."

"Just because—"

"Candy, it's all right. I didn't mean to cause any agitation on your part. So just relax . . . and enjoy your coffee."

She frowned at him over her cup. "You're a master of seduction and I don't trust you in the slightest."

"So it seems."

"You were very underhanded about getting me to go away with you last weekend."

"I confess I took a calculated risk. It was the only way I knew to be able to spend some time with you, to have you get to know me better."

She thought about that for a while before commenting. "You just seem so practiced at that sort of thing, that's all."

"I've told you that I'm willing to make any commitment you want from me. I meant that."

She nodded. "All right. Then let's work on a friendship. That's all I want from you."

"Friendship?" he repeated as though the word was unfamiliar to him.

"I'd feel much more comfortable."

Cade worked hard not to say what he was thinking about his comfort or lack thereof whenever he was around her. "Whatever you say."

"Good. I'm glad that's settled. If you don't mind I'd like to go to bed. I'm really tired. Must be all that fresh air and sunshine today."

Cade showed her to one of the guest rooms and bid her good-night. Then he went back downstairs and stared into the empty fireplace. Was this going to be his punishment for having a reputation where women were concerned?

Obviously.

Was she worth waiting for?

Absolutely.

Eventually he returned upstairs and went to another wing of the house to sleep. He hoped that was far enough away from Candy for her comfort.

"Candy?"

Candy fought her way through a heavy sleep. Drowsily she murmured, "Yes?" without opening her eyes.

Ariel drifted closer to the side of the bed.

"It is time, you know," Ariel said, her voice little more than a sigh wafted on a breeze.

"Time?"

"You have spent much of your life proving yourself to those around you. It is time now to take the next step in your development."

On some level Candy knew she was dreaming, but she was intrigued with the conversation. "My development?"

"Of course. You don't believe that your life is to revolve around your career, do you?"

"Well, yes, I guess I do."

"Oh, no. There is so much more waiting for you, once you conquer your fears."

"I'm not afraid!" Candy said strongly.

"Of course you are. Do you see how many of your decisions are based on fear rather than making choices that give you an opportunity to experience the joys of life? It is very important that you understand this. Cade Callaway is no one to fear. He will not harm you. It is you and your fear that will create the most pain for you. If you do not believe me, watch what happens if you continue to push him away from you."

"Why am I so afraid?" she whispered to herself.

"You have deeply buried many scenes from your childhood, my dear, but they continue to influence you."

"What scenes? What have I buried?"

"Cade reminds you of your father. Remember how he was, Candy? A good-looking man who charmed all the ladies with his flirtatious banter. You witnessed the quarrels between your parents, your mother's pain when women showed up at the door looking for him. You decided at a very young age not to trust men who reminded you of your father."

"I don't remember any of that."

"No. You blocked it from your memory, but the hurt and the pain you felt for your mother is still there. You've developed a strong need to protect yourself, but it is time to let go. Otherwise, it will be your loss."

Ariel's voice grew more and more faint until the room was silent once more.

When she woke up the next morning, Candy had forgotten about the unearthly conversation she'd had the night before. She felt rested and was ready to greet the day that included Cade Callaway.

There was no one in the dining room when she arrived downstairs. She wandered over to the coffeepot and was pouring a cup when Maria came through the doorway from the kitchen.

"Good morning," Maria said. "What would you like for breakfast?"

"Oh, I'll wait for Cade."

"He ate hours ago. They're having some trouble with one of the bulls this morning. The bull got out of his pen sometime last night. Cade and the others are trying to get him back inside."

"Oh. Are they nearby?"

"No. The pens are some distance from the house."

So Candy had breakfast alone, then spent her time wandering through the downstairs part of the house. Despite its size, the place had a very warm, comfortable feeling of home. Eventually she found a magazine and was glancing through it when she heard a commotion in the hallway.

"Easy there," someone said urgently. "Don't jostle him. Maria, call Doc Simmons. Cade's been hurt."

Candy didn't recognize the male voice speaking, but she certainly understood his words. Tossing the magazine aside, she ran for the doorway to the hall.

She gasped at the sight. Three men were carrying Cade on some type of crude stretcher.

The man giving orders must be Maria's husband, she thought. He directed them to take Cade into one of the rooms at the end of the hall.

"What happened?" she asked, horrified to see how pale and still Cade appeared.

The man glanced around. "I don't think it's serious, but I'd rather the doctor decide that. The bull charged him, grazed his side and knocked him into the side of the pen. Cade hit his head on the steel gate and was knocked unconscious."

She followed them into a sunny room that looked as though it was a children's playroom and watched as they carefully lowered him onto a daybed.

Candy found the adjoining bathroom and splashed cold water on a towel. She returned to Cade's side, seeing that the blood on his shirt was coming from a head wound. As quickly as she could, Candy wiped the cut clean, then put pressure on it to stop the bleeding.

She knew that head wounds bled heavily and could look more serious than they were. She fought not to panic as she stared down at the man lying there unconscious, looking so pale.

If she'd ever wondered about her feelings for this man, they were no longer in doubt. The thought that something could happen to him, that he might have been killed, was too devastating to imagine.

"Cade? Can you hear me?"

His eyelashes flickered, then slowly opened.

"Cade?"

He stared at her for a long moment, then closed his eyes. She began to cry.

Maria hurried into the room with water and bandages. "The doctor will be here soon. How is he?"

"I can't tell. He opened his eyes, but didn't say anything."

"Don't upset yourself," Maria said practically. "Here. Let's get this shirt off him and try to make him more comfortable."

With practiced skill Maria unfastened the shirt and slid it off his shoulders. Then she bathed his face and chest with careful gestures, much as a mother would a child.

"These things happen all the time here," Maria said briskly. "It is very dangerous work these men do. No matter what modern equipment they use, working around these large animals is a risk because the animals are unpredictable."

She began to speak in a low voice to Cade, checking to see if the bleeding had stopped.

Candy found a chair and sat down before her legs gave way. Why hadn't she understood all of this before? What had she thought he did for a living, anyway? She'd assumed that with the money the

Callaway family had, that Cade had his men do the dangerous work.

Seeing him unconscious made it clear that he expected as much of himself as he did of others. This was no playboy rancher with nothing to do but cultivate his social life. Hadn't he told her that this was his life?

It occurred to Candy that it wasn't Cade she doubted as much as it was herself. She had made love to him because it seemed the most natural thing for her to do. Then she had been too frightened of what he made her feel to continue with the relationship.

He could have been killed today. How would she have felt about her need to keep him at a distance then? Why was it that she felt she had all the time in the world, when her world could easily be destroyed by a recalcitrant bull on the loose.

Somehow, she had to let Cade know that she'd been wrong, very wrong, not to follow her heart. The future was never guaranteed. All anyone ever has is the here and now.

Chapter 16

The next time Cade opened his eyes, he kept them open and looked around the room.

"Candy?"

"I'm right here," she said, stepping to the end of the bed.

The doctor sat beside the bed looking at Cade. "I swear you've got the hardest head of anyone in these parts, bar none, Cade. You're probably going to have the granddaddy of all headaches for a couple of days, but other than a slight concussion, I can't find a thing wrong with you."

Cade's smile was a little shaky. "Thanks for the encouragement, Doc," he said before his eyes found Candy again. "Sorry about messing up your visit."

She fought to control the tears that came to her eyes. "You haven't messed up a thing."

"What time is it?"

"Almost noon."

Cade glanced at the doctor. "I must have been out for a while."

"Probably needed to catch up on your rest."

"When do you have to go back to town?" he asked Candy.

"No time soon. As long as I'm at the office by nine in the morning, I'm fine."

"Good," Cade murmured.

The doctor stood. "I'm leaving you a few tablets for the pain, Cade. You know the drill. If you have any nausea, double vision, etc., give me a call."

"You mean this has happened before?" Candy asked before she could stop herself.

"It comes with the job description," Dr. Simmons said ruefully. "I thought Cade got his fill of bulls on the rodeo circuit."

Cade grinned. "That I did. But today couldn't be helped. We couldn't have this fella romancin' the gals without some restraint. He wouldn't know when to quit!"

Candy could feel her face flaming when both men chuckled.

"What happened to my shirt?" Cade asked, glancing down at his bare chest. He eyed Candy curiously.

"Maria took it off, so she could soak the blood-stains out as soon as possible," she explained. Maria had also covered him with a blanket so that only his shoulders were bare. "Shall I get you another one?"

He pushed himself up on his elbows, then groaned.

"I don't think you're going to be wanting to go anywhere just yet," the doctor said. "Stay quiet if you know what's good for you."

Candy followed the doctor to the front door, asking questions and getting instructions about Cade's care for her own peace of mind. When she walked back into the room where Cade still lay, she sat down beside the bed in the chair the doctor had just vacated.

"You really scared me," she began, stroking her fingers over his hand.

"I didn't mean to. This is definitely not the way I planned this weekend to go."

"I'm sorry you were hurt, but I'm glad I was here so I could better understand."

"Understand what?"

"What your life is all about. I guess I was refusing to look at what was happening between us. Maybe I thought I could just ignore my feelings and they would go away."

His gaze softened and he brought her hand up to his lips. "Tell me about your feelings, Candy-cane." He rubbed her fingers back and forth across his jaw.

"About that commitment you were talking about?" she began, then stopped.

"Mmm-hmm?"

"What I'm trying to say is—well—maybe I want a little more from you than friendship, after all."

"God, I hope so!" he said fervently.

"I hadn't realized what a coward I am, always playing it safe, refusing to take chances."

"You took quite a chance last weekend."

"Yes."

"Are you still sorry?"

"I was never sorry. Confused, maybe. Chagrined, perhaps. Completely over my head, without a doubt. You make my head swim, Cade."

"I can sympathize with that, all right," he said, carefully touching the bandage on his own head.

"I realize that I don't have any answers. I'm the original city girl, while you're definitely a country boy. My work is in law, while yours is here on the ranch. But we seem to have more important things in common than those things."

Cade's eyes were sending her all kinds of intimate, heat-filled messages while she stumbled through her explanation.

"Are you by any chance trying to tell me that you love me, Candy-cane?" he drawled. "If I'd known

I could get such a response from you, I'd a signed up for a round with that ornery bull before now."

"You're always going to be a tease, aren't you?" she whispered, before leaning over and kissing him very gently on his lips. When she raised her head, he was smiling.

"Guess it's just part of my nature," he admitted, not at all apologetic. "I seem to delight in teasing you, at least. Maybe it's because you take life so seriously. I can't resist ruffling your feathers from time to time."

"Cade?"

"Mmm?"

"You have my permission to ruffle my feathers anytime you want. I'm tired of fighting my feelings for you." She kissed him again, this time with a lingering thoroughness that left them both a little breathless.

"Does this mean you'll marry me?" he finally asked.

"If that's what you want."

"Yeah. That's what I want. Soon?"

"I haven't given the idea much thought."

"I don't want a big wedding. I just want you...now...in my arms and in my bed. I love you, Candy. I'll do whatever you want. If you want a splashy wedding, I'll do it. But in the meantime, I want you to move out to the ranch with me. I don't want to give you a chance to change your mind."

She smiled at him. "It would never happen."

"Have you ever thought about commuting by air? We've got a helipad already on the ranch. We'll just schedule your flights with the main office."

"I don't think we need to concern ourselves about that just yet."

"Remember, you could be pregnant," he said. "Don't you think we should go ahead and get married now? We could always do some kind of family reception later, when the folks return from Europe. What do you say?"

"The doctor said to keep you calm and happy, so I guess I'd better agree to any suggestions you make," she replied, suddenly feeling as though she'd cast off her old cares and concerns.

Cade Callaway was her future and she was more than willing to let her future begin right now.

PART III
Matt

Chapter 17

Matthew Callaway was in his office working on a trial brief when he heard a commotion in the reception area of his law office. There were sounds of raised voices and a baby crying. He heard his assistant say, "You can't go in there," just as his office door flew open and bounced against the wall.

A young woman stood there with eyes flashing, a small child in her arms, glaring at him while muttering, "Oh, yeah? Well, watch me!" She charged across the large room toward him as he hastily rose to his feet.

"May I help you?" he asked more in astonishment than with any real degree of sincerity.

"Oh, I think you've done more than enough," the woman exclaimed. She marched around his desk and deposited the screaming child in his arms. "She's your blood, Mr. High-and-Mighty Callaway. You help deal with her!"

Matt knew that his past was not unblemished. After all, he'd raised himself on the streets of San Antonio until he'd become a teenager, but he'd had an opportunity to change his perspective about life and his role in it during the years since then.

He knew for a fact that he had never seen this woman before in his life. If he had, he would have definitely remembered her. She would have stood out in any group.

She wore her long, very thick black hair pulled away from her face where it cascaded over her neck and shoulders in a tumbling mass of glossy curls and waves. Black eyes were busy shooting daggers at him while he shifted his gaze in numb disbelief between the unknown woman and the child in his arms. The child had now stopped crying and was studying him with unfeigned interest.

The woman was tiny, barely reaching his shoulder. She wore a colorful dress with a southwestern flavor that played up her exotic good looks.

No. He'd definitely remember if he'd ever laid eyes—or hands—on her before.

The little girl squirmed in his arms. She wrapped one arm around his neck and patted his cheek with her other hand. "Da-da!" she exclaimed, chortling.

"No! I mean . . . Look, young lady—" He wasn't at all certain which one of them he was addressing, "I couldn't possibly be your da—this child's father. What's going on here?"

"I'm sorry, Mr. Callaway," the receptionist said from the doorway where she and his assistant stood, showing signs of agitation. "I tried to explain to her that she would have to make an appointment, that you were extremely busy and wouldn't be able to—"

"Never mind, Mindy," Matt said. "I'll deal with this." He sounded much more optimistic than he felt. He looked at the woman. "Please, have a seat." And to Mindy, "Would you please close the door and hold my calls?"

"Certainly, sir."

The response came from Mindy, not the black-eyed woman, who at least had followed his suggestion and was seating herself across from him.

Matt knew nothing about children and had no intention of learning anything about them. He was determined to get to the bottom of this. He sat down very gingerly as though he were holding a very sensitive bomb in his arms, one which could go off at the slightest jarring.

"Who are you and what are you doing here?" he asked, grabbing the little girl's hand to prevent her from exploring the contents of his shirt pocket.

She switched her attention to his open collar, suddenly finding a treasure trove of soft fine hair growing beneath the shirt.

"Ouch!" Matt cried, convinced the child was multihanded and feeling a distinct loss of control of the situation.

"I don't like this any more than you do," the woman said, "but I have nowhere else to turn. So you're just going to have to help me."

He managed to disengage the child long enough to put her on the floor, where she promptly took off running, headed for his potted plants in the corner.

"Oh, my God," he said, racing to head her off. He whisked her off her feet, which caused a spontaneous cascade of giggles to erupt from her. He turned to the woman sitting there watching him so calmly. "Help me out here, will you?" he demanded.

She eyed him for several long moments before holding up her hands and saying, "Come to Mommy, Emma."

The little girl laughed and vigorously shook her head. *"No."*

"I doubt that I need to explain where she gets her stubbornness, do I?" the woman said with a smile.

"If your method of getting in to see me is any indication, I would say it's quite obvious," he replied.

He walked over and unceremoniously dumped the little girl onto the woman's lap. "Now, who are you?"

"My name won't mean anything to you."

"Try me."

"All right. Jill Anderson."

He took his time walking back around the desk and sitting down. "And the purpose of your visit?"

"My daughter is two years old. I've just discovered that Emma has a very rare blood type. The doctors tell me that she's going to need surgery to correct a problem, but won't schedule it without having an adequate supply of her blood type on hand. I suppose I could search out others with matching types, but it would take time, and if there are family members with that blood type it would provide the insurance Emma needs."

"What does that have to do with me?"

"You have the same blood type."

"What makes you think so?"

"Because you're a Callaway... and so is she."

"Ah. I'm beginning to understand. Are you saying that one of the Callaways fathered your child?" He wondered what Cade and Clint had been doing three years ago and if this woman was going to throw a monkey wrench into their present relationships.

Jill quickly disabused him of that particular notion.

"No," she replied. "I'm saying that one of the Callaways passed on the blood type to my father. Although I don't have it—it seems to have skipped my generation—I've discovered that Emma does."

"Can your father—?"

"My father is dead, Mr. Callaway. He was already in his fifties when I was born. He's been gone almost two years, now."

"Who was your father?"

"Arthur Anderson."

"I thought you said he was a Callaway."

"That's right," she nodded emphatically. "He was. He was given up at birth by some member of your family who didn't want him. He was adopted by John and Martha Anderson."

"Is this what he told you?"

"No. My father never discussed it with me. I'm not certain that he knew the truth. I discovered the adoption papers by chance in an old family Bible I found tucked away in a forgotten corner of the family home. He was no longer alive by then for me to ask him about them."

"Do you have the papers with you?"

"Yes, I do."

Now they were getting somewhere. "May I see them?"

She reached into her handbag and pulled out a large manila envelope, wordlessly offering it to him.

Matt took the envelope, but didn't open it. Instead he kept his gaze on her. "What is it you are hoping to accomplish by coming here today, Ms. Anderson?"

She held his gaze for a long moment, then looked away. He could see the stiffness slowly leave her shoulders and she gathered the little girl closer against her.

Emma now rested her head on her mother's breast. Her eyes fluttered closed. "I've always known about you people. Anyone living in Texas can't avoid hearing about the Callaways. You seem to seek publicity, the way you're always being written up somewhere. When they told me that Emma needed this surgery, I didn't know which way to turn. Then I remembered these papers. I knew my dad's blood type was different from anyone else in our family. I didn't understand why until I discovered he was adopted." She met his gaze once more, her eyes glaring. "You can't know how sorry I am that I have a drop of Callaway blood in my veins. Believe me, if there was anything else I could do, I would. I need you to donate some blood."

Matt leaned back in his chair. "And why did you come to me?"

The look she gave him made her thoughts of his question rather clear. She had a very expressive face, Matt noted. "You're a Callaway. You're a lawyer. You represent the family in legal matters. I don't want to turn this into a legal battle if I can help it. Emma needs the operation soon. I make my living as an artist, which doesn't pay much. I can't afford to be tied up in court for years, even if I had the money to hire a high-powered attorney to face you." She nodded toward the envelope lying on his desk. "So I thought if I showed you the proof, it would save time."

"As it happens, Ms. Anderson," Matt said with a lopsided smile, "if you are, in fact, related to the Callaways then you are more of a Callaway than I am. I was adopted when I was fifteen years old."

Her eyes rounded in surprise. "Are you serious?"

"Extremely. I consider myself to be very fortunate, given the circumstances. Perhaps your father did, too."

"As I said, we never discussed it."

"Have you discussed any of this with your mother?"

"No. She left when I was about Emma's age. I have no idea where she is and I don't care."

"I understand that sentiment, as well."

"Surely one of the other Callaways would help me if I could convince them of who I was. Who should I see?"

"You were correct in thinking that I represent the family. Actually you brought these papers to the right party. Unfortunately I don't have time right at the moment to look them over. If you'll give me a number where I can reach you, I'll give you a call when I have finished studying them and we'll discuss the matter further."

"If you think you can destroy them and get rid of me like that, think again. Those are copies. The originals are in a bank safe-deposit box."

"Good for you. You're protecting yourself and that's smart. However, I have to finish this brief tonight to present in court first thing in the morning. Your papers will have to wait."

"Is there someone else here in the office who can help me?"

He thought of Candy, but dismissed the idea. He would have to consult with Cade about all of this as soon as he had an opportunity. It would be up to Cade how he wanted family information to be disclosed.

"No."

She studied him for a long time before sighing. "All right." She rattled off her phone number. "I'll be waiting to hear from you."

He smiled. "I never doubted that for a moment."

Chapter 18

Matt finished the brief about nine o'clock that night. He had one of his assistants standing by to put it on the computer so that it would be in final form when he returned to the office the next morning.

He let himself into his condo through the garage, feeling the weariness of a long week catching up with him. He'd been in trial since Monday. They had recessed at noon today—Thursday—to prepare for a ruling requested before trial resumed in the morning. He was thankful he'd researched most of it before Jill Anderson had exploded on the scene.

Once she was gone, he'd laid her envelope with its bombshell information aside while he wrote up what he had so carefully researched. Now, he was ready to deal with whatever information it contained.

"That you?" Cade called from the den.

Matt paused in the kitchen long enough to pour himself a hearty shot of bourbon over ice. "And if it wasn't me, what were you going to do?" he asked, strolling into the den where Cade sat with his feet propped up on the coffee table.

"I must have left my trusty six-shooter at home, so I guess I'd have had to wrestle a would-be burglar to the ground," Cade replied with a grin. He raised a long-neck bottle of beer in a silent toast. Matt returned the gesture and swallowed some of the bourbon.

Matt sank into his favorite overstuffed recliner and sighed.

"Rough day?"

Matt chuckled. "I'd already decided that it was rough before a two-year-old girl attempted to explore the contents of my shirt pockets and my chest hair."

"You sounded a little harried when you called, I must admit."

Matt still held the envelope in his hand. Once he was aware of it, he tossed it to Cade. "See what you think while I just relax for a few minutes."

Cade straightened, his feet falling to the floor. "Have you looked at it?" he asked, turning the envelope in his hands.

Matt closed his eyes and rested his head on the back of his chair. "Nope."

"No curiosity?"

"About what?" Matt lazily replied.

"Which Callaway might have given away a baby so many years ago?"

Matt opened his eyes and sighed. "Not particularly. It wouldn't have been anyone I know."

Cade leaned forward. "I've been thinking about this ever since your call this afternoon. If it's true, then something was going on way back in my grandparents' time. I've been enjoying working on the journals and legal documents I found stored at the ranch. It's like getting to know your relatives all over again. My dad's parents died when he was twenty. Mom lost both her parents before any of us were born. I guess I could sympathize with this woman— what did you say her name is?"

"Jill Anderson. She's an artist of some sort."

"I can understand her wanting to know more about her own family."

"She didn't seem particularly enamored with the idea that she shared anything with the Callaways."

Cade tapped the envelope against his palm. "I've been wondering if my dad knows anything about this."

"You don't think he's involved, do you?"

Cade chuckled. "How could he be? Depending on how old Jill's father was, I would think he and my dad were about the same age. Wouldn't it be something if they were brothers?"

Cade finally flipped open the clasp on the envelope and pulled the papers out, spreading them across the coffee table. "They all look legal enough," he mused, glancing at them. "I don't see any name but Anderson." He looked up at Matt. "I thought adoptions were supposed to be handled without either party knowing about the other."

"All that depends on whether it was a private adoption or done through an agency. If this was a private adoption there's a chance the parties already knew each other." Matt reached over and picked up a couple of the documents. "I would say that since these papers didn't surface until after Arthur died, they may have been kept private, even from him."

"So how did this woman find them?"

"She said she recently came across an old family Bible."

"Hmm. Look at this. There's a signature here that's almost unreadable." He frowned, trying to read. "The ink's really faded, but I think I do make out the name of Callaway." He glanced at Matt. "This really feels strange."

Matt nodded. "I know. At least I knew who my mother was. Not that I was any better off knowing."

Cade stopped reading. "You're so much a part of this family, I forget that you were adopted. I can't imagine what it would be like without you." When Matt didn't comment, Cade went on. "So what do you suggest we do about this woman?"

Matt took another sip of his drink and sighed. "Give her some blood, perhaps?"

"Now there's a ghoulish suggestion."

"That's all she says she wants."

"What about her husband? I take it his blood can't be used."

"She never mentioned him."

"Well, look. Why don't you bring her out to the ranch Saturday? Remember I told you that Clint and Gabrielle are flying in tomorrow for the weekend? It might be fun to get to meet our newest relative. Then we can find out what it is she needs from us. I don't mind donating blood for a worthy cause, but I admit I'm more curious about who this woman is and what her claim is on the family."

Matt sat listening to Cade's enthusiasm with irritation. "Why should I have to bring her? Why don't you?"

"Because you're here in town. I assume she lives in San Antonio?" After a pause, he said, "I know, I know. You didn't ask. But she did give you a phone number. The thing is, it would make the situation simpler if you were to escort her out there. Otherwise, she might not be able to find the place."

Matt rolled his eyes. "Travel with a small child? I can hardly wait."

"Don't be such a grouch, Matt. You know, it wouldn't hurt you to develop a social life."

Matt stared at him in horror. "With a two-year-old?"

"I was thinking of the mother. You said she was a striking woman."

"I said I thought she was going to strike me there for a while. Compared to her, a whirlwind would seem like a summer breeze."

"That's my point. You need something to shake up your life a little. You've turned into a workaholic over the years."

"So?"

"You should lead a more balanced existence."

"I do what I like to do. I'm good at what I do." He glared at Cade. "Just because you finally got Candy's attention doesn't mean that everyone needs to have a relationship."

"Fine. Then enjoy growing old alone. I don't care. In the meantime, bring Jill Anderson to the ranch tomorrow so we can meet her." He stood. "It might improve your disposition if you'd go on to bed before you spend the night in that chair. I'll let myself out."

Matt woke up the following morning with a start. He'd been dreaming about Jill Anderson, of all people. This time she hadn't had a child with her and the erotic things she'd been doing to him in the dream were illegal in some states.

What was going on with him, anyway? Maybe he'd been too obsessed with work lately. He knew this trial had taken all of his time and energy. Hopefully they'd finish up sometime next week. Perhaps he needed to take a few days off after that. He could go down to Corpus Christi and do some fishing, or lie out beside a pool somewhere and vegetate.

From the content of his dream, he needed some female companionship, as well.

Matt forced himself to focus on the issues he wanted to argue at the early-morning hearing while he showered, shaved and dressed. After a hasty breakfast, he headed to the office, getting there before any of the staff.

The first thing he did upon arrival was to call Jill Anderson. As soon as she answered, he knew he'd awakened her. His body reacted to the sound of her husky, sleep-edged voice.

"Ms. Anderson?"

"Yes."

"This is Matt Callaway. You were in my office yesterday."

She seemed to come awake. "Yes?"

"Some of the Callaway family would like to meet with you this weekend. Would it be convenient for you and your husband to come with me to the ranch south of San Antonio tomorrow?"

"I don't have a husband, Mr. Callaway."

"Oh."

"When do you want to leave?"

"How about noon?"

"Fine. Where shall I meet you?"

"I can pick you up at your home if that would be more convenient for you."

"Okay." She gave him her address and directions how to get there, which he dutifully jotted down. "I take it that you believe my story."

"I never disbelieved it, Ms. Anderson. If you'll excuse me, I need to go to court. I'll see you tomorrow."

"Fine," she said, hanging up.

Jill stared at the phone beside her bed for long moments after she'd hung up. What was it about Matt Callaway that caused her to react so strongly to him? Was it because he reminded her of Steve, Emma's father? If anything, that should be the biggest turnoff she could have.

Maybe she was just one of those women who never learn. Big, blond, blue-eyed men were going to be her fatal attraction. Matt Callaway was definitely an attraction she could do without.

Long before she'd found the papers about her father, Jill hadn't cared for the Callaway family. They seemed to think they were some kind of Texas royalty. They probably owned half the state . . . at least they acted as if they did.

Well, she didn't want anything to do with their money. The whole situation would be amusing, really, if she weren't so worried about Emma. The Callaways no doubt found it easy to pay off any debts of a personal nature with cold, hard cash. She wondered how they felt about being asked to donate blood?

Chapter 19

After spending another restless night filled with erotic dreams involving Jill Anderson, Matt woke up the next morning in a rotten mood. It didn't matter what name he carried, he knew he wasn't a Callaway. Cade might be able to forget that he was adopted, but Matt never could.

He would always be an outsider and he knew it. Oh, they all treated him well enough. The invitation to visit the ranch in order to see Clint was sincere and some part of him appreciated the casualness of the offer. It was true that none of the family treated him any differently than the others.

But he knew that he didn't belong. He'd followed in his adoptive father's footsteps by becoming a lawyer. He knew he was good at what he did. He took pride in it. But this morning he couldn't think of anything that he disliked more than the idea of showing up at the ranch with this Jill Anderson and her child in order to find out where on the Callaway family tree she fit.

He just hadn't found a way to get out of it.

Matt followed the directions Jill had given him and found himself in an older part of town. The house must have been built before the Second World War, but looked to have been carefully maintained.

When he pulled into the driveway and got out of his small sports car he felt as though he'd stepped back in time. Large shade trees lined the narrow street. The homes had been built around the same time and had similar features. Most were wooden with large front porches and a single car detached garage. Some places were filled with flowering shrubs and flower beds, while others had carefully tended lawns.

It wasn't at all what he had imagined would appeal to Jill Anderson. But then, what did he know about her, come to that? That she could fight like a tigress for her young?

He strode to the front steps of the porch, taking them two at a time. He'd barely knocked on the screen door when the wooden door behind it swung open.

At first he didn't recognize her. Then he looked again. Gone was the colorful sprite who'd charged into his office. Today was a girl who didn't look much over fourteen. She wore her hair in a single braid tossed over her shoulder. She had on an oversize sweatshirt and snug-fitting jeans.

She carried Emma on her hip.

Emma began to bounce and sing, "Da-da, Da-da-da-da," with a lilt.

"Stop it, Em. You're managing to embarrass both of us," Jill said, looking anything but embarrassed. She glanced at him calmly, with more than a hint of amusement. "I wasn't certain if this was a command performance or not."

"I beg your pardon?"

"Am I supposed to dress as though I'm being presented to royalty?" she asked.

Matt glanced down at his own Western-cut shirt, jeans and Western boots. "If it is, nobody bothered to tell me."

"Oh, it wouldn't matter where you're concerned. You're family."

"If those papers are valid, so are you."

She looked up at him appraisingly. "You think I'd make them up?"

"It wouldn't make any difference. Blood tests are easy to arrange. Either the Callaways can help you or they can't." He opened the screen door and Emma fell into his arms, jabbering in a tongue that didn't have the slightest resemblance to English.

Jill picked up a tote bag and her purse, then stepped outside and closed the door behind her, locking it. Only then did she notice his car.

"Now there's a mean-looking machine. Why am I not surprised that you'd be driving something so powerful?" She showed no intention of taking back her daughter, so Matt resettled Emma onto his arm and shoulder and followed Jill down the steps to his car.

She walked all the way around it, admiringly. "My dad would have loved your car. He was a real nut about autos and racing." She paused by the passenger door and waited while he opened it for her. He looked down at Emma.

"Does she have a car seat?"

"Oh! Yes. Hold on, I'll go get it." She raced off toward the garage, leaving him holding her inquisitive daughter, who was presently doing her best to wriggle out of his arms.

He almost dropped her before he got a better hold on her.

Jill hurried back with a regulation car seat, which Matt installed behind the front seat of his car. The area was small but adequate as he placed the little girl in the seat, and fastened her in.

"Do you have children of your own, Mr. Callaway?"

"No."

"Then how did you know about—"

"I know the law, Ms. Anderson. I've seen what happens to children who are in automobiles without protection."

She smiled and slid into the passenger seat, carefully fastening her seat belt. "That's right. You're an attorney, after all."

He closed the door and walked around the car, then climbed inside. He'd always liked this car, but he'd never been so aware of its lack of size before. Jill's arm was only a couple of inches from his. Her knee rested against the console where he would be changing gears. The light scent she wore permeated the small interior of the car.

This had not been a good idea. Not at all. He would have a few words to say to Cade as soon as he saw him.

Matt concentrated on getting through San Antonio and out on the highway while Jill appeared content to ride along without conversation. In fact, she appeared more relaxed than he felt.

Once they were south of the city Matt asked, "What sort of surgery does your daughter need?"

"Corrective surgery between her bladder and kidneys. I understand that it's something many of the women in her father's family have experienced, though the doctor has said it is not congenital."

"Does her father live around here?"

"No."

She certainly didn't give much away. When she didn't say more, he asked, "Does he see his daughter often?"

She slowly turned her head and looked at him. "What do you want to know, Mr. Callaway? Was I married to her father? Yes, I was. Was I sorry I married him? You'd better believe it! Would I prefer never to have met the man? Since I can't imagine what my life would be like without Emma, I'd have to say no."

"I'm sorry if it seemed as though I were prying."

She sighed. "You're a lawyer. You can't help asking questions. It comes with the territory."

"Do you know many lawyers?"

She laughed. "See what I mean?"

"Sorry," he mumbled. When nothing further was said, he decided to prod her some more. "Don't you have any questions you'd like answered?"

"Such as?"

"Such as, who you're going to meet today and their connection to the family…why I'm taking you to the ranch instead of having a meeting at my office…that sort of thing."

She didn't answer right away. When she did, her attitude surprised him. "I'm not particularly interested in the Callaways, either the people or their holdings. I suppose some people are in awe of your power in this state. You probably have women fawning over you all the time, but I honestly don't care to have more to do with any of you than is necessary to help Emma."

"You keep including me in the group."

"Why shouldn't I? It's your name, isn't it? It's who you are."

Matt could feel his muscles tense as he strove not to allow her remarks to get under his skin. He took his time before replying. "Callaway is my name. It is not who I am. I believe I mentioned to you the day we met that I was adopted. I don't know who my father was. I never knew what my mother's real name was because she used so many, depending on what she thought she could get. So, yes, I'll admit I enjoy having a name—any name. I took this particular name because the man who turned my life around, the man who literally took me off the streets and gave me a home, was a Callaway."

He glanced at her and saw that she was watching him with an expression on her face he couldn't interpret.

"You obviously have an aversion to the name," he said, "and I'm certainly not going to attempt to change your mind. But a name tells you nothing about who a person really is. I've met dozens of Callaways since I became a part of the family. There's no two of them alike." He paused and thought about that for a moment, then smiled ruefully. "All right, so that's a slight exaggeration. The two you're going to meet today look astonishingly alike because they happen to be twins. But their appearance is deceiving in that they are very different individuals.

"If, as it appears, your father was a Callaway, he may have been very much like the others, either in appearance or perhaps he had some of their personality quirks. Then again, he may have been nothing like them. You haven't asked for my advice, Ms. Anderson, but I'm offering it anyway. You might want to withhold judgment until you get a chance to meet these people. Who knows? Without all your prejudices, you might discover they're just people like you and your daughter, instead of ogres who are out to do harm to others."

Matt realized that somewhere in the course of his comments he'd become almost heated in the defense of his adopted family. He was surprised to discover that he had jumped to the defense of people who certainly didn't need him to rally to their cause.

He said nothing more. Instead he concentrated on his driving, doing his best to ignore the woman beside him. When she spoke after several miles, he was surprised at the change in her.

"I've really behaved badly and I'm sorry," she said in a low voice. "My father would have been appalled by my rude behavior toward you when you have been nothing but kind to me. He certainly didn't raise me to act this way. I really have no excuse. I guess I was scared and angry and I took it out on you."

Damn. He hadn't wanted to see this vulnerable side of her. He was much better off dealing with her more abrasive side. He gave her a quick glance out of the corner of his eye. "Don't worry about it."

A silence fell between them once more. A half hour must have passed before Jill broke the silence between them.

"Are there really identical twins at the ranch?"

"That's right," he replied.

"How old are they? Are they still in school?"

Matt laughed. "Hardly. They're my age."

"Oh! I guess I pictured them still living at home."

"One of them lives at the ranch and oversees the operations there. The other one works for the government out of Washington."

"Oh, dear. Have my accusations stirred up a hornet's nest? They're bringing in reinforcements?"

"Not at all. Clint just happened to be visiting for the weekend. Both of them are intrigued by the mystery you've presented us. I gave Cade, the other twin, the papers you brought to my office. He planned to spend yesterday digging through the attic to see what he could find to substantiate what you've brought to our attention. Unfortunately none of the surviving members of the family were alive back when your father was born."

"I've often wondered if he knew he was adopted. He was one of the most gentle and kindest men I've ever known. Unfortunately I grew up thinking that all men were like that. My marriage taught me otherwise quickly enough."

"I'm sorry that you had to experience such a lesson."

"I'm not. It made me grow up. I guess I was too much of a daddy's girl before then."

Matt saw the familiar gates of the family ranch and began to slow down. "Emma has certainly been quiet since we got in the car."

Jill flashed him a brilliant smile. "I know. Isn't it heavenly? Car rides are like a narcotic on her. Two blocks away from the house and she's out for the count, which makes her much easier to deal with when I have to go somewhere."

He turned in between the two stone pillars and followed the blacktopped road through the hills.

"Thank you for bringing me out here, Mr. Callaway. I had no idea the ranch was this far from town, or as large as this."

"Do me a favor, okay? Call me Matt. Otherwise, it's going to get confusing in a little while with all the Callaways around."

She smiled. "All right...Matt. And I'd appreciate if you'd call me Jill."

Eventually they arrived at the main house. Matt pulled up in front of the entrance. By the time he was out, Jill had gotten out on the other side and was busy getting Emma out of the car seat.

When he walked around to her side of the car to help her, all he saw was a well-shaped rear in snug jeans. Jill eventually straightened, her face flushed with the exertion of getting her daughter from his car. Without considering what he was doing, Matt automatically held out his arms to take Emma from her, just as though he'd been doing it for years.

Chapter 20

As soon as the introductions were made, Matt showed Jill and a restless Emma where the rest rooms were. She and Emma disappeared down the hall while the twins and their mates went into the den.

"She reminds me of someone," Clint said, settling on the sofa with his arm stretched along the back behind Gabrielle. "But I can't think of who."

Cade nodded. "I was thinking the same thing. Of course we've been going through family pictures so much, it could be anyone. I've almost gone cross-eyed looking through so many photos and papers that belong to the family."

Candy spoke up. "At least Gabrielle's theory seems to have solved the who of this story." She smiled at the other woman. "Must be her training. She knew just what she was looking for."

"*Her* training! What about me? I've been in the business longer than she has," Clint said in an injured tone.

"But you're too close to the family to be objective," Gabrielle replied, patting his arm in mock consolation.

Just then Emma came running into the room ahead of her mother. Ignoring the other four people sitting there, she made a beeline for Matt, arms outstretched.

"Looks like you've made another conquest," Cade commented from where he sat sprawled on the floor at Candy's feet.

Matt could feel his face flushing, which was ridiculous. All of them were strangers to Emma, except him. Naturally she would search out a familiar face.

He leaned over from where he sat and picked her up, placing her on the wide arm of his chair, his arm wrapped securely around her.

"This is a beautiful home," Jill said from the doorway. There was no defensiveness in her face nor tone.

The men hastily scrambled to their feet. Cade was the first to speak.

"I know it looks like a hotel sitting out here in the hills, but when you round up all the family, we need this much room." When Jill continued to stand just inside the doorway, he added, "C'mon in. We were just discussing the situation regarding your father's adoption."

"Oh?"

She came in and sat down next to Gabrielle. The men resettled in their seats.

"What's Gabrielle's theory?" Matt asked, interested despite himself.

"Gabrielle pointed out that it had to have been a Callaway woman who placed her baby up for adoption. Otherwise, the Callaway name wouldn't be on the natural mother's papers."

"That makes sense," Matt replied.

"So that narrowed our search considerably. There would be no reason for our grandmother to give a child away. And there was only one other female Callaway around." He waited expectantly, but when Matt continued to stare at him blankly, the twins chorused, "Aunt Letty."

Matt began to laugh. "Now wait a minute. I knew Aunt Letty. There's no way she could have anything to do with this."

Clint spoke up. "I thought the same thing, but once Gabrielle mentioned it, I could see that she would be the logical choice. The four of us searched the attic for any of Aunt Letty's things."

"And?" Matt prompted.

Cade shrugged. "And we didn't find anything pertaining to an adoption."

"Why doesn't that surprise me?" Matt replied.

Gabrielle smiled and said, "Actually we did find something of interest that may still guard her secrets, if she ever wrote them down. What we found was the desk she used to keep in her room. Clint recognized it when he saw it."

"So?" Matt couldn't see how a desk would have any connection with a possible adoption.

"I think if we search her desk diligently enough, we could find a journal or something that she may have written," Gabrielle said.

"The thing is," Cade said pointedly, "I've already gone through Aunt Letty's household journals. There was nothing personal in them."

Candy spoke up. "I agree with Gabrielle. From what we've discovered so far, Aunt Letty kept such meticulous household details, it is hard to believe she wouldn't keep some record of such a huge event. I believe she kept a hidden journal, and we're convinced it's somewhere in that desk."

"You know how they used to make those things with all the little hidden drawers and things?" Gabrielle asked, looking first at Matt, then at Jill.

"Yes," Jill said, nodding. "My dad had one that he said belonged to his parents. I used to have fun playing with all the hidden springs and catches. He and I used to leave messages for each other in them all the time."

The two couples looked at each other, then back at her.

"You're just what we were waiting for," Cade said, scrambling to his feet. "Would you be willing to show us what to look for?"

Jill looked a little taken aback by his enthusiasm. "Well, if it's anything like the one I have, I can. But there were all kinds of desks made back then."

Matt stood, still holding Emma who seemed perfectly content to be in his arms. "I think they've got the right idea, Jill. At least you know the kind of secret drawers and things that were made...where they might be placed, and so on."

"Do you think Emma would stay with Maria?" Cade asked Jill. "It's really dusty in the attic. Maria's very good with children, by the way. She's in the kitchen at the moment. I bet she could tempt Emma into sampling some of her baking."

Emma clung to Matt for long minutes after he'd taken her to see Mrs. Ramirez, but gradually the toddler was coaxed out of his arms to explore the wonderful smells coming from the cookie tins.

"I'll be happy to watch her for you," Maria assured Jill. "There's no problem."

Once in the attic, Cade led the way to one of the corners. The light switch at the door to the attic controlled a row of ceiling lights so that there was plenty of illumination. He paused by a small *secrétaire*.

"Oh, how pretty," Jill said with awe.

"Is it anything like yours?" Cade asked.

"It's much smaller."

"Do you think it has any hidden drawers?"

She knelt beside it, pushing on various knobs, pressing bars, before she looked up at the sea of faces around her. "I don't see anything."

"What about that?" Matt pointed to a small indentation at the edge just below the writing surface.

She shrugged. "I've never seen anything like it."

Matt pressed, then slid his finger over the area. A small, shallow drawer opened several inches out of what looked like solid wood. A slim journal lay inside.

"This must be how Sherlock Holmes felt," Cade drawled, causing them all to laugh.

"Let's go downstairs and see what's in it," Clint suggested.

Jill could have stayed there for hours, looking around at the pieces of furniture, the storage chests, the toys—all those things collected over the years by a family with a place to store their treasures.

She followed the others downstairs and went looking for her daughter.

"I turned her over to my daughter," Maria said with a smile. "She's playing with her in the toy room. Would you like to see?"

Jill followed Maria down another corridor and into a sunny room. It was a child's wonderland. She shook her head in amazement. Emma saw her and started talking, holding up a stuffed bear.

"I see that," she said softly. "Are you having fun, Emma?"

"Uh-huh."

"Well, Mommy will be here if you want me."

Jill had a hunch she wouldn't be missed anytime soon.

How strange not to have to be concerned about Emma. She'd been so used to being on her own that she found it difficult to adjust to the idea that strangers were helping to ease her burden for a few hours.

She returned to the den where all of them were waiting for her.

Cade spoke. "I didn't want to start without you. I'm going to read this aloud so we'll find out if she mentions anything about a baby. Is that okay with you?"

Jill nodded. They were already treating her as one of them. How strange.

The journal was thin with a heavy backing in a green-and-black swirl design. Cade flipped it open and began to read from the faded ink of a very fine, flowing penmanship.

Today is the first day of classes and our English professor suggested that we keep a journal in order to write down our thoughts and feelings now that we've arrived here at school.

I don't need to write them down to remember them. I really hate this place and wish Mama hadn't insisted that I come here to college. Why couldn't I have gone to school in Texas, where I belong?

The girls here make fun of me—the way I talk, the way I dress. You'd think they'd never seen a pair of cowboy boots before! They're the ones who look silly with all their laces and ruffles. They look ridiculous. And the stuff they put on to ride horses make them look like a bunch of ninnies.

They even make fun of the way I ride. I don't care anything about their English style of riding and their stupid saddles. There's not a one of them who could ride a horse bareback if she had to.

I'm going to write Mama weekly as I promised I would. I'm also going to write Grant, since he's overseas fighting.

Cade paused and looked around at the three women sitting there. "That was our grandfather's name—Grant. He and Aunt Letty were brother and sister." He glanced back to the book and continued reading.

I worry about him and I miss him. I wish I were a man. I'd be off fighting, too. I don't want to be a nurse and they're the only women over there.

I feel so useless here. They make such a big deal about the proper way to sit, to walk, to hold a fork and set a table. Everything's so blasted proper. Sometimes I want to let out a loud Texas yell just to get some life into the dorms.

I'm going to ask Dad to ship me my own saddle. I don't care what they say, I don't intend to learn how to ride that sissified way. They look like a bunch of idiots posting around the paddocks that way.

"Just think of the adjustment it must have been for her to leave the ranch and go to school back east," Candy said softly. "It must have been like going to a foreign country to somebody raised on a ranch back then."

Gabrielle spoke up. "I was looking through her household journals, and she didn't strike me as the kind of person to waste time on nonessentials."

"That's true enough," Clint replied. "She was tough as a boot. In all the years I knew her, I never saw her in anything but boots and jeans, but the really strange part was that I never saw her on a horse. Yet here she is talking about riding as though that was her favorite thing to do in all the world. I guess that just proves that we do change as we get older. What appealed to her as a young girl no longer interested her in her later life."

Cade said, "You know, this reminds me of something I heard my folks talking about, years ago. Mom was upset about something that Aunt Letty had done and Dad said it was due to the way Aunt Letty had been raised. He said she was treated like the princess of the palace here on the ranch. As the boss's daughter, whatever she said was treated as a royal edict. I bet she was really ticked to have to be treated as just one of the group back east."

"Especially if they were making fun of her," Candy added.

"Does she talk about dating anyone?" Gabrielle asked.

Cade read ahead. "Nope. Once she got her own saddle, and wound up with a room of her own, it looks as though she didn't bother with this journal much. There's just a few notes here and there about classes." He turned a few more pages. "Ah. Here she is, coming home after graduating from college."

It's wonderful to be home once more. I can't believe how much I've missed this place. Summers and holidays were never long enough here.

Mama, Dad and I had the most wonderful surprise three days after we got home from my

*graduation—Grant came home. What a tre-
mendous graduation gift!*

*What's even more exciting is that he's home
to stay. He got a medical discharge. He insists
that he's much better now and that eventually
he'll be as good as new.*

*Nobody had told me that he'd been wounded.
I can't believe they kept something like that
from me! At first all I wanted to do was follow
him around the place, making sure he was really all right.*

The twins looked at each other. Clint cleared his
throat. ''That doesn't sound like the old prune we
used to know, does it?''

''Uh-uh,'' Cade replied gruffly.

''There's so much love and warmth there. Whatever could have happened to it?''

''I don't know.'' Cade turned a page, then exclaimed, ''Wow, here's a mention of our other
granddad—Mom's dad! He must have worked here
on the ranch at the same time Letty was here.''

He picked up the narrative once more.

*Grant brought a friend home with him. His
name is Antonio Alvarez. They met in basic
training and spent their whole military career
together. Grant says that when you get a couple*

*of Texans together in the same unit, they know
how to set an example for the whole platoon.*

*Tony's originally from Harlingen, down near
the southern tip of Texas. Grant told Dad that
he'd like to offer Tony a job here on the ranch,
that if it wasn't for Tony, he wouldn't be alive
today.*

"I remember hearing that story from Dad, don't
you, Cade?" Clint said. "He said his father used to
talk about how Tony saved his life, risking his own
life by helping Granddad Callaway to get back behind our lines after he'd been hit by enemy fire."

"I know Grandfather Alvarez was always a hero
in Mom's eyes," Cade replied. "She talked about
him so much...about how gentle he was with her.
He'd wanted a large family but there were some kind
of complications when Mom was born so they never
had anymore. She said she used to ask him if he
wouldn't have rather had a son and he'd scolded her
for even suggesting such a thing. Long after Grandmother died from cancer he would never consider
marrying again, Mom said. Mom wondered if he
would have lived longer if he'd had someone else.
She said when Granddad Callaway was killed, Tony
just seemed to give up caring much about life."

"Hell, he had enough reason, didn't he?" Clint
said. "Besides the shock of his best friend being
killed, a week later, according to Dad, dear old Aunt

Letty fired him from the place he'd worked and lived all those years." He nodded toward the book. "Maybe she'll tell in there what she had against him."

They listened while Cade continued to read the words that Letty Callaway had written all those years ago.

Tony just got back from visiting with his family in South Texas. He's been gone for three weeks. While he was gone I helped Grant clean up one of the cabins that's been sitting empty for years. It was fun to turn an old storage place into livable quarters.

Grant teased me because I wanted to hang curtains over the windows and hang some pictures on the walls. I told him that Tony needed something over the windows, and at least curtains let in a little light. They aren't frilly ones. I made them from leftover material from the curtains Mama had made for Grant's room. If they aren't too sissy for him, then Tony should like them just fine.

The pictures give the place a nice homey feeling. There's one of a snowy mountain scene with a wolf howling at the moon. There's another one, a Remington print, of an Indian on his pony. They give the room character. I made

Grant promise not to tell Tony I helped to decorate.

Cade turned over several pages and began to read once more.

It doesn't seem possible. Tony's been working for us for almost a year. He and Grant spend most of their time together. Dad's really impressed with how quickly Tony's learned what needs to be done around here. I heard Dad saying the other day that he's thinking seriously about making Tony foreman, that is, if he intends to stay here.

I hope he stays. I really like him. He's always so polite with me. He laughs at my jokes and he's even teaching me how to speak Spanish. Tony says I'm a natural at picking up the language and pronouncing the words correctly.

Sometimes I look in the mirror and see why all the girls in college made so much fun of me. I don't look feminine at all. I'm tall and skinny with none of the curves where most of the other girls have them. Mama says I'm built more like her sister. I don't think that's fair. Why couldn't I have been beautiful like Mama? Then maybe Tony wouldn't treat me like Grant's kid sister. Maybe he'd see me as a woman.

Cade faltered to a stop. He looked at Clint. "You don't suppose—?" He stared down at the journal without seeing it. "It can't be." He looked over at Jill, staring at her for a long while before he met Clint's gaze. "That's it, isn't it? We thought that Jill looked like someone in the family, and she does. But not a Callaway, Clint. Don't you see? She looks like Mom."

Clint nodded, his expression grave. "Those pictures of Mom when she was growing up here on the ranch. Remember? She used to wear her hair just like that."

Matt could think of nothing to say to ease the brothers' shock at this latest discovery. Jill studied her hands folded in her lap as though she had nothing to do with the present conversation. Gabrielle and Candy, as though understanding the need of the men they loved, touched them lightly. Gabrielle placed her hand on Clint's thigh, while Candy rested her hand on Cade's shoulder.

Finally Matt cleared his throat and said, "Don't leave us hanging, Cade. We might as well hear the rest of it."

Cade swallowed hard, then began to read once again.

Grant hurt his leg yesterday and he's laid up in bed today. I offered to take his place and Tony just laughed, but he let me ride with him. They were out riding the fence line, making sure the barbed wire was still strung and that there were no posts down. Tony admitted it was one of the most boring jobs on the ranch, but it was also one of the most vital.

He already had the horses saddled and our lunches packed when I got outside. It was barely light. As we rode out we watched the sun peek over the hills.

What a magical day today was. We didn't get home until almost dark and now I'm so tired I can hardly keep my eyes open, but I have to put all of this down so that I always remember this day. For the first time since he came here, I finally feel that I've gotten to know a side of Tony that he doesn't share with many people. I found myself telling him about school and how unhappy I was. He couldn't believe that I consider myself awkward and ugly. He told me so many things that I wish I could believe about myself. I would love to be the person he described to me.

Cade paused, then looked up from the journal. "It seems to end here," he said, turning the next page, then another one. "Oh. There's more here." He checked the dates. "This is several weeks later and her handwriting is harder to read, like she's writing fast or is upset."

"Read it," Clint said gruffly.

Cade nodded.

I will never ride again. I will never do anything like this ever again. How could I have been so stupid? So juvenile? What could I have been thinking of?

It all seemed so innocent at the time. All these weeks I've wallowed in Tony's attention, never thinking about what it all meant...all those compliments, the looks he gave me, the way he treated me.

We went riding today after he was through with work. It was so hot and he suggested we go down by the river where it was cool. I thought it was a wonderful plan. We would sit in the shade and listen to the water as it trickled over the stones.

It's my own fault, of course. I must have thrown myself at him. He must have thought— It doesn't matter what he thought. Not now.

I'll admit that I wanted Tony to kiss me. No man has ever kissed me in my life. I wanted to see what it was like. I have no excuses to make for my behavior after that. It was as if some other woman took over, some heathen with no morals at all.

It hurt at first, but at the time I didn't care. I was no longer thinking about anything. When it was over Tony started saying all these things to me...how he loved me, how he hadn't meant for this to happen. How he had wanted to wait... how he wanted to marry me.

It was then that I truly realized what I had done. I'd thrown away my virtue like the lowest type of female there was. I'd had carnal knowledge of a man that I had no intention of marrying.

He was the hired help! How could a Callaway possibly consider such a thing?

Today has been the most horrible day of my life. I have sinned against God, against my family, against myself. Because of my reckless behavior I have chosen to give up what I enjoy the most—I will never ride again. That is my bargain with God. That is my punishment.

Tony didn't understand why I wouldn't listen to him talk about marriage. I had to finally tell him the truth. I would never marry a man like him, a laborer on my father's ranch. I am a Callaway. He kept staring at me with those black eyes of his, looking at me as though I had suddenly turned into a foreign creature of some sort.

He never said a word after that. He was very polite. He helped me on my horse, but he never looked directly at me again.

Cade couldn't read any longer. This was his grandfather she was talking about. His *grandfather!* He was half-Alvarez and half-Callaway. What in the hell was wrong with that?

Cade looked at Clint disgustedly. "What a stupid old bat," he muttered. "She deserved all the unhappiness she got. Granddad loved her and wanted to marry her, for hell's sake!"

Clint nodded. "I remember Mom once saying that she and her family were never good enough for Aunt Letty, but that it never really mattered to her because all the rest of the Callaways accepted her. Mom's mother and Dad's mother were close friends, she said."

Matt said, "It would be interesting to know where Letty got all her ideas. Who knows? Maybe she learned that at that eastern girls' college."

"Or maybe," Gabrielle suggested quietly, "that was the armor she donned in order to deal with all the hurts she received while she was away at school. Except that she ended up convincing herself that it was true."

Candy leaned forward and asked Cade, "Is that all that's in there?"

Once again Cade flipped through several blank pages, pausing when he came to more writing. Without looking at the others, he began to read . . .

I've convinced Mama that I'm totally bored on the ranch these days and that I want to go visit with some school friends. She assumed that I was talking about some of my college friends and I allowed her to think that. However, the truth is that I wrote Bessie Mae Kingsley, now Tuttle, and asked if I could come visit for a while. She was my very best friend in the third grade until her family moved to East Texas.

I told Mama when Bessie's reply came that it was an invitation to visit, which was the truth. I just didn't tell her the invitation was extended at my request.

I'd only been at Bessie's two weeks when she recognized what was wrong. Why shouldn't she? She's already got three of her own. I told her that nobody at home knew and that no one would ever know. I intended to find a home for it as soon as it arrived. I also told her that I had found a room at a boarding house in town where I could stay until the baby was born. I told Mrs. Harrell, who owned the boarding house, that I was recently widowed and would be returning east once I could travel again. I don't care if the old biddy believes me or not. She took my money. Why should she care?

I miss the ranch. And Grant. And my parents. Mama writes regularly, which is a help. I'm always vague about my plans to return as

*though I might be home by next week. It's get-
ting harder coming up with excuses for wanting
to stay so long. But it won't be much longer
now, the doctor says.*

*I've had all these months to think about my
life and my future. I know that I will never
marry. I could never let another man touch me.
I just couldn't. Sometimes I wonder if Tony
misses me or whether he hates me for what I did
and said.*

*I am on my way home now. I feel as though
I've been gone six years rather than six months.
I know I feel years older than the person who
traveled east months ago.*

*They brought him to me that first night. I
guess nobody told the night nurse that I
wouldn't be keeping my baby. She woke me up
and silently handed him to me.*

*I took him. How could I not? It would be the
only time I would ever see my precious son.*

*I couldn't believe how much hair he had. I
snipped a tiny piece from the nape of his neck.
No one will ever notice. He lay there in my arms
looking up at me with those big, dark eyes,
studying me as much as I was studying him.*

*He has Tony's coloring but his eyes are
shaped like Mama's, so big and beautiful. I'd
never seen a baby that small before. But he was
perfectly formed.*

Now I understand how God's punishment works. He wants me to live, to remember that I have a son that I will never see again. He wanted me to look into my son's eyes, to fall in love with him, then to tell him goodbye. That is my punishment.

It would have been far easier to have died in childbirth.

Chapter 21

Cade closed the journal and laid it on the table beside him. Nobody spoke.

After a long silence Gabrielle said, "God didn't punish her," she said, her voice cracking slightly. "God doesn't do things like that. He's a loving, understanding, compassionate God. He understands humans. He knows we're not perfect. Letty punished herself. Her pride was more important to her than love. It's obvious that she loved Tony. She's so hard on herself and on him. From the sound of things, he never knew about his son."

Another silence filled the room. After a while Candy said, "It must have been so hard on her to keep such a terrible secret to herself. She lived with it all of her life. No wonder she grew to be the kind of person you've described. She went through life never forgiving herself. No wonder she had such a tough time being tolerant of other people's flaws."

Clint nodded. "I was thinking about how it must have been for Aunt Letty when Granddad finally married someone else. She had to watch him with his wife, and then his daughter, for all those years. I wonder if she ever regretted not telling him about the baby, or if she wished that she'd accepted him when he proposed."

Matt leaned forward. "The question is, what are you going to do with that journal now that you've found it? Are you going to show it to your folks?"

The twins looked at each other in dismay.

Jill surprised them by speaking for the first time. "I can't tell you how ashamed I am for what I've done."

They all looked at her in surprise.

"Matt mentioned earlier that I shouldn't allow my prejudices to blind me toward people. I finally understand what he was talking about. I knew nothing about the Callaways, but I had a definite opinion about who and what they were. Finding the papers about my dad strengthened that belief. Today, I've seen your pain as you learn something about your family's past that was better off remaining hidden."

"Not necessarily," Clint interposed. "As long as it's the truth, we need to face it."

"But at whose expense?" Jill asked quietly. "From what you've said, this information would be devastating to your mother, who has a firm sense of who her father was."

"There's nothing here to change that," Cade said quickly.

"No. But you know, yourselves, that you will never think of Tony Alvarez and Letty Callaway the same way again. There was no reason for you to know any of this. Unfortunately I didn't understand that until it was too late. I was so wrapped up in my own problems and in Emma's health, I gave no thought to what this would do to any of you."

Matt felt a distinct sinking sensation in the pit of his stomach. He'd been fighting the strong physical attraction this woman had for him, but her admission just now caught him off guard, fully engaging his emotions. It couldn't have been easy for her to speak up at this time. The fact that she'd had the courage to do so touched him much too deeply for his own comfort.

"There's no reason to let anyone else know about this," Matt said. "As I understand it, Jill needs blood donors for her daughter's surgery. It sounds as though you two—" he looked at Clint and Cade "—would be the obvious ones to help her out. You share Callaway and Alvarez blood. The other family members don't need to know that Jill is related to you."

"Yes," Jill said, "That's very true. I promise that I'll never bother any of you again." She nodded toward the journal. "I think we should get rid of the journal and the papers I discovered. All those people are gone now. Why disturb the ones who are still living?"

Clint stood and looked around at the gathering. "I don't think we need to make a decision anytime soon. The folks won't be back for a few weeks. The information has kept this long, hasn't it?"

Jill got up, as well. "I agree. I also need to get Emma home." She looked over at Matt. "If you wouldn't mind driving us back to town."

The others began to move. Cade quickly said, "You have to stay for dinner. It's another two hours before you get back to town."

Jill shook her head. "I appreciate the offer, but if Matt doesn't mind, I'd really like to go home now."

"I don't mind."

Jill turned and hurried from the room, saying, "I'll go get Emma."

After she was gone the two brothers looked at Matt.

"What?" he asked blankly.

The brothers looked at each other and grinned.

"I hate it when you guys do that," Matt said. "You're obviously communicating on some level the rest of us don't have."

Gabrielle chuckled. "It isn't all that hard to figure them out, Matt."

"Really?" He looked at Candy, whose amusement was obvious. "All right! So everybody gets it but me. What's going on?"

Candy very gently said, "She's a very attractive woman, Matt."

He could feel the hairs on the back of his neck stand straight up. "So?"

Clint draped his arm around Matt's shoulders. "All we're saying, old son, is that we think you work too hard and we'd like to see you relax a little, and enjoy life more."

Matt frowned. "Huh?"

The rest of them burst out laughing. They were still laughing when Jill reappeared in the doorway with her daughter. "I'm relieved to find everyone laughing. What's the joke?"

Matt scowled at the room at large and walked over to where she stood. "I have no idea, but I have a hunch that I'm the butt of it, whatever it is."

Everyone gathered around Jill and told her how pleased they were to meet her and Emma, and Cade invited her to return to the ranch anytime.

Matt couldn't get them in the car and away from there fast enough.

"Is something wrong?" Jill asked, once they were on their way. "You're awfully quiet."

"Just tired. I've had a busy week."

"I appreciate your taking your day off to bring me out here. You have a very warm and loving family."

"I know."

They didn't say another word for the rest of the trip back to San Antonio. It was dark when Matt pulled into the driveway. He got out and helped Jill to remove Emma and the car seat. Somehow, he ended up holding the sleeping child while Jill took care of the car seat.

She opened the front door and carried her purse and the car seat inside. Then she returned to take Emma from him. "Would you like to come in for a drink or something?"

Matt took a deep breath, reminding himself that he did not want to get involved with this woman. He knew the risks and he wasn't prepared to deal with them.

"No, I need to go on home."

Jill went up on her toes and placed a light kiss on his cheek. "Thank you for everything, Matt. I really appreciate your overlooking my behavior the day we first met."

His cheek stung where she'd touched him. He stood there staring at her stupidly, not knowing what to say.

"Good luck in court," she added, then stepped back into the house.

"Good luck with Emma" was all he could think of to say in reply.

Matt returned to his car and drove home on autopilot.

He wasn't completely certain of all the ramifications of Jill's visit to the Callaway ranch today. She'd been successful, which was the main thing.

There was no reason for him to have to see her or Emma again, which should make him feel much better.

But somehow, it didn't.

Chapter 22

Three weeks had passed since the visit to the ranch. During those weeks, Matt finished his case...and won...while at the same time did everything in his power to dismiss Jill Anderson from his mind...and lost.

He convinced himself, finally, that it was only natural that he would want to know what had transpired regarding Emma's surgery. With that in mind, he phoned Jill one morning.

No one answered.

Two days later, he called again.

No one answered.

After a few more days, he ambled down the hallway to Candy's office and found her hard at work.

"Something bothering you?" she asked, seeing his frown.

"Not really. I was just wondering what Cade did about little Emma Anderson."

"Oh! Didn't you know? She had her surgery on Monday."

Matt looked away, his jaw flexing. "Is she all right?"

"The surgery was successful, if that's what you mean."

"I, uh, tried to call Jill but there was no answer."

"I'm not surprised. I think she's staying at the hospital full-time until she can bring Emma home."

Making a decision, he asked, "What hospital?" Candy told him, then went back to work, effectively dismissing him.

What had she expected? That he should have known? That he should have kept in touch? Was she judging him because—?

Matt caught himself. He was putting all kinds of motives on her behavior that weren't necessarily true. Even if it were, he didn't owe her any explanations for his behavior.

Then he left his office and drove to the hospital, stopping at the florist on the way.

As soon as he walked into the hospital room, Matt realized he'd miscalculated. The tiny plant and balloon he was carrying were dwarfed by the number of floral arrangements and toys sitting around the room.

Then his gaze went to Jill and he forgot everything else. "When was the last time you had any sleep?" he demanded gruffly, trying to keep his voice down because Emma was asleep.

"I catnap when I can," she replied. She'd risen as soon as he walked in, her surprise at his appearance evident. "What are you doing here?"

"I just found out that Emma had surgery on Monday. Why didn't you let me know?"

Her puzzlement was as plain on her face as the deep shadows beneath her eyes. "It never occurred to me. Cade and Clint both donated blood and I sent them thank-you notes and mentioned that she'd gotten through her surgery very well. I didn't think you—" She must have seen something in his face, because she stopped speaking.

He walked over to Emma and lightly touched her hand. "She looks so tiny lying there. When she's awake she's so full of energy it's hard to remember how small she actually is."

Jill joined him beside the bed and smiled down at her daughter. "I know. She constantly amazes me."

He stepped away from the bed, fighting the emotion that had swept over him as soon as he'd walked into the room. He wandered around the room looking at the flowers. He noted that Cade and Candy had sent some, as had Clint and Gabrielle.

"You could open a flower shop with all of this," he said, feeling unneeded and in the way.

"I've been touched by the outpouring of their concern for someone they don't even know all that well."

He stopped his restless circling of the room and faced her. "Will you do me a favor?"

"What's that?"

"Will you go home and get some sleep? I'll stay here with her, so she won't be alone whenever she's awake."

"Oh, I can't let you do that. You need your rest. As busy as you are, I'm sure that—"

"—I can survive missing a few hours sleep. You, on the other hand, are going to fall over in your tracks if you don't go to bed soon."

They stared at each other across the room—two strong-willed, determined people. Jill's gaze was the first to fall. "If you're sure..." She didn't seem to know what more to say.

"I'm very sure. I will be here by her side until you return. Now go home and get some rest."

Her eyes filled with tears and before he realized what he was doing, Matt had his arms wrapped around her. He held her close to him, luxuriating in the feeling of having her in his arms. This was much better than any of the dreams he'd been having since he'd first seen her.

He wondered when was the last time someone had just held her. He could feel her tears soaking the front of his shirt. She was exhausted and had no doubt been running on nothing but reserves all week. Now even that was gone. She was so independent and so strong. Had it occurred to her to ask for help?

Only once, when she'd needed the insurance of blood for her daughter. He could see how out of character her behavior had been. She wasn't used to accepting help from anyone.

She wiped her eyes with the back of her hand, much like a child. He lifted her chin and placed a kiss on each eyelid, on her nose, both cheeks, and finally on her mouth. She gave a little sigh and relaxed against him.

Matt lost track of time and of place. This was what he had needed for so long. Why had he fought it so?

Reluctantly he pulled away from her and, taking her by the shoulders, turned her around to face the door. "Now go."

In the following hours he grew accustomed to the hospital routine. Emma woke and fretted, but seemed to be eased by his presence. The nurses came in and out, as well as the resident doctor, who explained the procedure that had been done on her and discussed the time she would need to recover fully.

Sometime after midnight Matt was resting in the large chair that must have been where Jill had been sleeping all week when he heard the door open.

One of the nurses came in…a new face. No doubt there had been a change of shifts. She came over to Matt rather than looking at Emma, which surprised him.

He glanced at her name tag. How unusual. There was only one name—Aramis.

"Thank you for coming," she said, her voice as light as a bird song on the summer air.

He straightened in the chair as though to get up, but she motioned for him to keep his seat. He settled back. "I wanted to be here," he admitted in a low voice.

"Yes," she said softly, "I know. But you were afraid."

Startled by her bluntness, he said, "What do you mean, afraid?"

"When we are hurt at a very young age, it is difficult to open our hearts and give or receive love. We guard ourselves. It is the only way we know how to survive."

He looked at her more closely. Had she gone through such a trauma as a child? It was difficult to tell. She didn't look all that old, actually.

"I suppose," he admitted. "I don't think I've really missed anything, though."

"Almost. You almost missed something." She nodded toward the little girl. "She needs you, you know. She needs to learn about love, not only from her mother, but from a father as well."

"Whoa, now, wait a minute. I'm not in the market for a family, thank you very much."

"It is time, Matthew," she said gently. "You have no place to run because you've been running from yourself and your feelings. You must forgive your mother for her lack of care and nurturing. You need to understand that she was incapable of caring for anyone, including herself. She didn't live long after you ran away that last time. She didn't make it to thirty, my dear. She gave you life, Matthew, which was a very important gift."

"You knew my mother?"

"Let us say that I was aware of her struggles. She loved you very much. Her problem was that she could never forgive or love herself. And it eventually destroyed her."

Matt was startled to feel tears on his cheeks. He couldn't remember the last time he had cried. Not since he was a very small child.

He had a sudden vision of his mother, one of the few times in his life that he recalled where she was happy. Now that he thought about it, she was happy because it was his birthday. He couldn't remember how old he was.

"Three," whispered Aramis and he nodded in agreement.

When he was three, his mother had looked like an angel to him, with her flyaway white-blond hair and her large, deeply blue eyes. It was her eyes that he could recall most vividly from that day. They were filled with love and laughter.

"She loved me," he murmured to himself.

"Oh, yes. Very much."

He felt as though he were choking on unshed tears. "I never knew."

"I know. It is difficult for a child to understand all that is happening around him. You were protected, of course."

"Protected?"

"Oh, yes," she replied serenely.

"I was living on the streets, foraging for food out of Dumpsters. That isn't much protection."

"But you were safe from harm when most children on the streets are not. You learned very quickly to look after yourself. Now it is time for you to learn how to look after others."

He looked over at the bed. "You mean Emma?"

"And her mother. Jill will never tell you how much she needs you. She's been hurt very badly herself. She's learned not to trust the kindness of others. But you can change all of that for her."

"How?"

"By being here for her and her child, just as you chose to be tonight. This was a big step for you today, coming to the hospital, agreeing to stay here. You moved out of your safe place and have allowed yourself to feel something for others. I am so proud of you."

"Why do I feel so much pain in my chest?" he asked.

"All of that suppressed emotion is there bursting to be released. Let it go, Matthew. Let it go. Grieve for your mother, my dear, as she grieved for you. Allow yourself to feel all the love and admiration stored in your heart for Cameron and Janine Callaway. Loving another person isn't a sign of weakness. It is a sign of strength. It is time for you to be strong, Matthew. It is time."

One moment he was sitting there talking to the nurse, the next moment he was alone. Matt blinked his eyes, then rubbed them. He got out of the chair and went over to the door. Opening it, he looked out into the hallway. There were three nurses at the pediatrics' station and two passing one another down the hall. None of them looked like Aramis.

He closed the door and went back to the chair beside the bed. Maybe he'd been dreaming.

That was it. He must have been dreaming. How would a nurse have known about his mother, about the Callaways, about his fear?

But why would he dream such a thing, especially when he hadn't been thinking about his family. He'd been sitting there reading about the latest earthquake to hit the continent of Asia.

He'd ask Jill in the morning if she'd ever spoken to a nurse named Aramis.

Chapter 23

"I can't thank you enough for helping me to get Emma home," Jill said to Matt when she brought the little girl home from the hospital. "It's amazing how much stuff we managed to accumulate during her stay."

Matt carried in the last stuffed animal and potted plant, looking around Jill's living room. "Where shall I put these?"

"In any available space you can find. I'll deal with them later."

This was the first time he'd been in her home, although he'd seen her each day at the hospital. Emma took his presence for granted, but Jill continued to act surprised every time he walked into the room.

It was obvious that Jill took very little for granted.

At least he'd gotten her into the habit of going home at night to sleep. She was already looking much better than she had the first day he saw her at the hospital.

Matt stuck his hands into his pockets, feeling terribly unsure of himself. "Why don't I go get some takeout so that you don't have to prepare a meal this evening?" he asked when Jill returned from checking on Emma.

"Oh, that's all right. You've already done so much. I can't keep taking advantage of you this way."

"Well, I have to eat, too, you know. And I kinda hate eating alone." He'd never really thought about that before, but it was a true statement.

"Well, if you're sure..."

"I'm positive. Tell me what you like and I'll go get it."

When he returned she was asleep on the couch. He shook his head in exasperation. She still wasn't taking care of herself the way she needed to. He was going to have to do something about that.

After he found dishes to put everything in, he set the table, poured them some tea and returned to the living room to wake her up. On impulse he knelt beside her and kissed her.

She slowly opened her eyes and blinked sleepily at him. "I fell asleep," she said sheepishly.

He grinned. "Like Sleeping Beauty."

"Yes. And you woke me with a kiss."

"Mmm-hmm."

"Are you a prince?" she asked, smiling mischievously.

"I would like to be . . . for you," Matt replied, his voice sounding like gravel to his ears.

"Why have you been so good to us, Matt?" she asked, lightly touching his cheek with her hand.

"It's easy being good to you two, Jill. I have a hunch these last couple of years haven't been easy for you." He took her hand and pulled her from the chair, leading her into the kitchen.

He pulled out her chair and waited until she was seated before sitting down across from her.

Once they were finished with the meal, Matt said, "There's something I need to discuss with you."

"Oh?"

"The twins and I have been discussing the matter, and we would like to set up a trust fund for you and Emma."

"No."

"Just hear me out. After all, you're part of the family and—"

"No. I'm not part of the family. I can never be a part of it. Don't you see? I'm still a reminder of something that happened years ago. You and your family don't want me as a reminder of what happened. Besides, I need to get on with my life. Emma and I are doing fine. Really. I appreciate everyone's concern but I can't accept anything from you."

He sat and studied her for a few minutes. Finally he nodded. "I understand. I can appreciate your viewpoint because I'm outside of the family circle, as well." He glanced at his watch. "I didn't mean to stay so late." He stood. "Take care of yourself and Emma, okay? Call me if you ever need anything."

She followed him to the door. "Thank you, Matt. I don't know what I would have done without you these past few days and nights."

"Glad to be of service, pretty lady. 'Night."

He walked away from her without looking back. He'd gotten too close to her for his own comfort. What had he been thinking? He glanced at the door once he'd backed out of the driveway. She was still there, silently watching him. He felt as though he had narrowly escaped making a complete fool of himself. She would have laughed in his face if he'd told her how much he was beginning to care for her.

Thank God he'd had the sense to get out of there.

Jill watched him drive away knowing that she wouldn't see him again. She had heard the note in his voice when he'd left.

Which was just as well. He'd been in her life for days now and in her weakness she had allowed it. But no more. Emma was recuperating. It wouldn't be long until their lives had returned to normal and she could get back to work.

She checked on Emma one more time before preparing for bed that night. It was only when she had almost fallen asleep that she recalled the look in Matt's eyes when he'd left. He'd seemed vulnerable and very much alone. She must have been mistaken. He was a successful attorney, a part of a large, wealthy family. If he was alone, it was by his own choice.

"Well, counselor," Candy said to Matt several weeks later, "looks like you did yourself up proud on that one. The jury was behind you all the way."

They were leaving the courthouse on a Friday afternoon and Matt knew he should be feeling jubilant. After all, he'd won his client a tidy sum of money, hadn't he? That was the purpose of taking these cases, wasn't it? To win? To look good? To feel good about himself?

Well, it wasn't working. For whatever reason, he'd been in a slump lately.

"I think I need a vacation."

"I have a suggestion," Candy said.

"What's that?"

"Why don't you use the family condo on South Padre Island this weekend? Cade and I were down there a few weekends ago. It isn't as exotic as the

Virgin Islands, but I found it very restful. It might do you good."

"That's not such a bad idea, at that. I've been thinking about getting in some Gulf fishing. I suppose that's as good a place as any."

"The key's in its usual place. The cleaning company keeps it ready for visitors, so you should be all set."

"Will anyone else be using it?"

She laughed. "Who would that be? The family's still gone and Cade and I are spending the weekend at the ranch being lazy for a change. Go on and enjoy yourself, will ya?"

Slowly he nodded. "Thanks for the suggestion. I just may do that." He handed her his briefcase. "Would you drop this at the office for me? I think I'll go on home now and get an early start."

"See you Monday, partner," she replied, waving him off. As soon as she got to her car, she called Cade. "He bought it. He's already heading home to get ready."

"Congratulations. I didn't really think you'd be able to pull it off."

"I'm really worried about him. I've never seen Matt so distant and withdrawn from everyone. I was prepared to badger him about taking some time off, but he actually jumped at the chance to get away."

"I just hope we're doing the right thing, that's all. I don't like the idea of interfering in other people's lives."

"I know. How did things go for you?"

"It was the toughest sales job I ever pulled off, believe me, but she finally agreed."

"How about Emma?"

"She's right here with me, removing everything from the desk as fast as her fingers can fly."

"Hang on, honey. I'll be there to help out as quickly as I can."

"I don't mind. I'm enjoying the practice. In another few months, if our suspicions are correct, we'll have one of our own. Oh, I forgot to ask. How did the trial go?"

"We won, otherwise I don't think Matt would have gone. I think he wanted to do something to celebrate and I offered a suggestion that appealed to him."

"He'll either kill us or thank us by the time this weekend is over."

"He's just too stubborn for his own good, you know. Maybe this will help put him in a better mood. He's been an absolute bear for weeks now."

"I'll see you soon, sweetheart. Don't forget I love you."

She smiled. "The feeling's mutual, Callaway."

It was after ten o'clock that night by the time Matt crossed the causeway between Port Isabel and South

Padre Island. He'd made the mistake of calling the office only to discover several phone messages that needed to be returned, so he'd gotten a later start than he'd dreamed.

Not that it mattered now. He was almost there and more than ready to forget everything else. Candy had been right. This was what he'd needed—a change of scenery.

He couldn't for the life of him figure out why he'd been so restless lately. He'd never felt the need for company in the past. In fact, he'd preferred being alone. However, he'd lost his enjoyment of his work for some reason. It was no longer enough to keep him busy or content.

He'd spent more time playing golf these past few weeks than he had in years. At least the exercise had been good for him, even if it hadn't curbed his discontent.

Of course, his restlessness could be the result of missing Cameron and Janine. His parents. The people who had given him his name. He'd been thinking about that a lot lately. For the first time in his life he'd had the urge to sit down with his dad and talk to him about his childhood memories, something he'd refused to do in the past. For some reason, he had a need to unburden himself to someone, to share that feeling of having been cast off—abandoned, unloved—that seemed to haunt his dreams lately.

Which was absurd. Absolutely absurd. He was a grown man who needed no one, who wanted no one.

He pulled into the condo parking lot. After getting his bag out of the car, he locked it and went upstairs. The complex was quiet. Not too many people here at this time of the year. He let himself in and without turning on any lights walked into the bedroom he generally used when he was there.

Feeling the weariness of the lengthy day weigh him down, Matt tossed off his clothes and crawled into bed, almost groaning aloud at the sheer luxury of feeling a comfortable bed and pillow beneath him at last.

The early-morning light came through the windows the next morning, awakening him. He hadn't thought to close the drapes the night before. He sat up and yawned, stretching vigorously. Good time of the day to do a little fishing, he thought. He stood and walked over to the window and looked out.

Beautiful morning sky, just turning blue. The sun wasn't up yet. He'd make some coffee and sit out on the deck and watch the sun come up. He glanced to his left, where a glass door led onto the deck, and met Jill's astonished gaze, her eyes appearing to grow larger as she took in his naked state.

"What the—!" He made a diving leap toward the bed at the same time she jumped up from the chair where she'd been sitting and turned away from him. He fumbled for his jeans, tugged them up over his bare shanks and zipped them before he jerked the door open and stomped out onto the deck.

"What are you doing here!" he demanded.

She kept her back to him, gripping the railing in front of her. "I was invited to stay here," she said. "I didn't know anyone else was here."

"You can turn around, you know," he said in a quieter voice. "I'm dressed now."

She glanced over her shoulder, taking in his bare chest and feet, "Not so a person would notice," she replied.

"I'm sorry if I embarrassed you, Jill, but I had no idea anyone else was here. I'm sorry." He couldn't help noticing that she wore a sheer beach cover over a skimpy bikini. He could feel his body reacting to the sight of her so provocatively revealed. He turned away. "I'm going to make some coffee," he announced, disgusted with himself for lusting after the woman as if he were a horny teenager.

He was watching the coffee slowly dripping into the carafe several minutes later when he heard the sliding glass door in the living room open. He glanced up, then away.

"I'll get my things and get out of here," she said, pausing by the kitchen bar. "I didn't mean to intrude."

He felt as though he'd just knocked a baby bird out of its nest. "There's no reason to leave," he replied. "As you can see from the size of this place, there's obviously room for both of us here."

"I'm certain you've made plans for the weekend. I don't want to interrupt anything."

"What are you talking about? You think I've got somebody coming down here to meet me?" What a preposterous thought that was.

She looked away. "Don't you?"

"No, I do not." He paused, then tentatively asked, "Do you?"

"Of course not." She sounded insulted that he should suggest such a thing.

"Then why would you automatically assume that I would?" he asked, pouring himself a cup of coffee. "Want one?" he asked.

"Please."

He poured her a cup and handed it to her.

"I just assumed that you have some kind of relationship going with someone, that's all," she finally said.

"Nope. The last time I attempted such a thing, I got shot down."

"Oh. I'm sorry."

"You shouldn't be. You had every right to send me packing."

"Me! You're saying that *I* turned you down?"

"Well, let's just say you made it clear that my help was no longer needed in your life."

"I only meant— I mean, you'd already done so much for me and Emma, I just didn't want to take advantage of your kindness."

"If you knew me better, Jill, you'd discover that I'm never kind. I spent time with you and Emma because I wanted to be with you."

Jill looked around the room, then nodded out to the deck. "Why don't we sit out there for a while? There's something I really need to tell you."

She led the way, and he warily followed her. She sank into one of the low chairs used for sunning. He sat down nearby and waited.

"I want to tell you about Steve," she began, then stopped as though unsure what to say next.

Despite his best efforts, Matt could feel himself tense at the mention of another man. "Who is Steve?"

"My husband. You reminded me of him the first day I saw you."

He winced. "From the little you've said about him, I take it he isn't one of your favorite people."

"I deluded myself where he was concerned, that's all. I grew up knowing Steve and his family. When my dad became ill they were there to help me, Steve most of all. He convinced me to marry him so that he could stay there and look after both of us. Later, I found out it was because he thought Dad had money and he wanted it to start a business. When he found out that there wasn't that much, and what there was went to pay doctor and hospital bills, Steve left.''

"He left you and Emma?"

"Actually he didn't know—*we* didn't know—I was pregnant at the time. I heard later from his family that Steve moved to Alaska. Dad died about the time Emma was born. That's when I decided to sell everything and move to San Antonio.

"I fell in love with that house and the neighborhood as soon as I saw it," she said. "I'd gotten enough from the sale of Dad's place to pay for it outright. We're comfortable there. I manage to sell enough paintings to pay the taxes and insurance on it, as well as support us in a modest way. I never wanted money from the Callaways. I tried to explain that to you. It wasn't you I was turning away. It was the offer of money. Only that.''

Matt could feel the tension within him easing at her explanation. She hadn't rejected him. Not really. And she was here now, wasn't she? Looking at him as though she liked what she saw. She'd given him hope that maybe some of his feelings might be returned . . . someday.

"What do you paint?" he asked. He was unable to keep his eyes off her as she reclined on the long, low chair.

"Landscapes, mostly. Some animals. I have a degree in art and was actually teaching when Dad became ill. I quit to stay home to take care of him.

Then when Emma came along, I chose to remain at home with her until she's old enough to go to school."

"Do you recall us discussing Allison Alvarez that day when we were at the ranch?"

"Allison? Was that Tony's wife?"

"Allison was Tony's daughter. She's the mother of Clint and Cade."

"Oh. I never heard her name."

"She's also an artist. She does sculptures."

Her eyes rounded. "Alvarez? You mean, she's the sculptor who signs her things Alvarez? Oh, my gosh, I don't believe it! She's wonderful."

"Is it surprising that you who carry the Alvarez genes might be an artist as well?"

She laughed. "I guess you could call that a coincidence."

"I don't believe in them."

"You don't?" she asked a little uncertainly.

"No." He moved over and sat beside her. "I believe that we were supposed to meet, Jill, you and me. I believe that you're supposed to be a Callaway by name as well as by blood."

"Matt?" she said faintly, her eyes looking like a startled doe.

"I'm doing this all wrong," he said urgently. "I know you don't know me all that well, but I need you to understand my intentions. I want to marry you. I want to help you raise Emma. And if you're willing,

I want us to have more children. I'll give you as long as you need to get used to the idea, but someday, somehow, I want us to be a family together. I need you more than I've ever needed anyone in my life."

She looked into his eyes and once again saw the vulnerability, the hint of desperation that he tried so hard to cover. This time she had no desire to send him away. Instead she reached up and put her arms around his neck.

"Show me," she whispered. "Show me how much you need and want me."

His kiss took her breath away. She clung to him, feeling a burst of pleasure when he cupped her breast with his hand.

"Oh, Matt, I've been so afraid of what I've been feeling for you, afraid I was going to be hurt again," she finally managed to whisper.

He removed the top of her bikini and nuzzled her. "I've been terrified, myself. Why do you think I've been running so hard?"

She ran her hands across his chest and felt him shudder with need.

"If I don't get you inside—now!—we're going to make a spectacle of ourselves for everyone on the beach to see." He whisked her up into his arms and strode into the room he'd slept in the night before.

Matt knew that he was rushing everything, but his control had snapped. He'd fought the fierce attraction for too long. Now that she was making it clear she wanted him just as badly he couldn't allow another moment to pass without claiming her.

She pushed at his jeans, shoving them off his hips so that he was forced to pause long enough to kick them off. They were both laughing at their eagerness to be together by the time all items of clothing were gone and he was inside her, claiming her, loving her, cherishing her.

With such a spontaneous meltdown, their lovemaking could only become more intense and volcanic. Jill held him fiercely to her, depriving him of his ability to delay completion. Matt felt as though he exploded into a thousand pieces when he heard her call out his name with such love and passion.

All the walls he'd built around his heart came tumbling down. He cried out his release, clinging to her as tightly as she clung to him.

He lay there, dazed, his heart pounding like a runaway engine. He could feel her trembling in his arms. He adjusted his weight so he didn't crush her. "Did I hurt you, love? I'm sorry I was rushing you so."

Jill placed kisses along his damp jaw. "Oh, no. You didn't rush me, nor hurt me. Oh, Matt. I had no idea it could be like this." She sighed. "I had no idea."

He leaned up on his elbow and looked at her. "Do you have any idea how beautiful you are?"

Her eyes were luminous as she gazed back at him. "As long as you think so, that's all that matters."

"I do have one question, though."

"What's that?"

"What are you doing down here at the island?"

"Oh. Actually when Cade and Candy stopped by last week—"

"Stopped by where?"

"My place. They usually come to visit with Emma and me once or twice a week. Anyway, they were telling me about having been down here and how relaxing it was. Then they insisted that I needed to get away for a couple of days, myself. Cade made it seem as though I was doing them a favor to allow them to keep Emma for me."

Matt began to laugh.

"What's so funny?"

"How easily we were set up. You see, it was Candy's idea that I come down here for the weekend, as well."

"You mean they planned this?"

He glanced down at their intertwined bodies. "I wouldn't be at all surprised." Growing serious once more, he said, "You are going to marry me, aren't you?"

"The thought of marriage really frightens me, Matt. If you'll recall, I haven't seen any good examples of the institution so far. My mother didn't stay with my dad for long, and I've already told you about Steve."

"I know. I never had much of a homelife, either, not until I was almost grown. But once you get to know the Callaways, you'll see some solid relationships that have lasted years." He leaned back onto a pillow and pulled her over until she was lying on his chest. "I've kept my distance from all of them for twenty years. I only recently understood it was because I was afraid that even people as loving as the Callaways wouldn't be able to love me. But I was wrong. They've been showing me their love and support for years, if I had only recognized it."

"It's going to be awkward, having me in the family, isn't it?" she asked.

He gently rubbed away the furrow between her eyebrows. "No. You will be my wife. We're Callaways, darlin', like it or not. Somehow they managed to get their brand on both of us. It's just something we'll have to live with."

"You know, I'm glad we found that diary. I mean, it's sad that Letty and Tony never had their chance together, but if they hadn't been together, if she hadn't become pregnant, then my dad would never have existed and I wouldn't be here now."

"I've thought a lot about that diary, myself. How misplaced pride can cause so much anguish. I guess I didn't need the Callaway blood to have the pride. I realize now that I was denying myself any possibility of happiness by not pursuing you."

"So what should I say to Cade and Candy when I go pick up Emma tomorrow?"

"We will pick up Emma together. I don't think we'll need to tell them anything, do you?" He kissed her lightly, then once again more slowly. "In the meantime," he whispered, "I've got a few suggestions on how to spend the rest of the weekend together."

He left no doubt in Jill's mind exactly what he had in mind.

Chapter 24

Allison Alvarez Callaway and her sister-in-law, Janine, sat at one of the many umbrella-shaded tables near the pool located on the Callaway ranch. Both women were avidly watching the whirl of activity going on all around them.

When the Callaways gave a party, it was an event not soon forgotten.

Allison leaned toward Janine, her eyes dancing. "Can you believe all of this? If I'd had any idea this would be the result of an extended European vacation, I would have suggested going away five years ago!"

Janine laughed, her face glowing. "I know. I'm still pinching myself to make certain I'm not dreaming."

Just then a group of children went running past them, laughing and screaming at the antics of one of the boys.

"How did we ever survive having children that age and hang on to our sanity?" Allison asked facetiously.

"I don't know, but it's certainly fun to watch as the younger parents try to cope with all that youthful exuberance."

"The joys of being a grandmother. We can enjoy them without having to take on the full-time job of guiding them to adulthood."

Janine nodded toward the barbecue pit. "Who would have believed when those two were growing up that they would end up getting married at the same time?"

Allison followed her gaze to where Clint and Cade were busy checking the progress of the roasted spit. "Why should anyone be surprised? Those two have been in competition since the day they were born. Now there's a bet going as to who will become a dad first. From the smug look on Cade's face, I would guess he thinks he's a definite winner."

Janine smiled. "Well, they both lose. Just look at Matt. If that isn't the look of a besotted papa, I don't know one."

Emma was standing beside Matt, holding on to his finger while she took in all the commotion around them. The young miss was definitely independent, yes, but not ready to completely let go. Give her time, though, and she would be joining them in the midst of all the commotion.

Janine continued. "Both Cam and I had given up the thought of Matt ever finding someone to love. He's always been such a loner, burying himself in his work. It does my heart good to see him so happy."

"I'll admit I was shocked to see what a difference it makes to see him smiling," Allison replied. "He's always looked so austere, even at family gatherings. He's taken all the teasing from everyone with such good grace, I've been absolutely amazed." She waved at one of the children who waved back.

"I can't tell you how pleased I am that all of them decided to say their vows today in front of the family," Janine admitted. "I know that civil ceremonies are legal, but having the pastor marry them adds something special to the vows, at least to me."

"Have you noticed the similarity in the personalities of the women our Callaway sons have chosen for their mates? The men certainly aren't going to have it all their own way in these marriages," Allison said, chuckling.

She sobered, remembering the night she and Cole had returned home. She'd been so excited to see her family gathered at their house waiting for them when they arrived. Cole had phoned ahead to let them know they were on their way home.

Only Clint had been unable to be there. He'd been away on an assignment at the time. However, the rest of them had been there—Tony with his family, Katie with hers and Cade with his brand new wife had greeted them with laughing exuberance.

She had missed them so much.

It was the next morning that she'd received the news that had shaken her world.

Everyone but Cade and Candy had returned home the night before. Cade waited until after breakfast before saying, "There's something I need to show you, as well as tell you. Could we go into the den?"

Allison couldn't ever remember a time when Cade had looked so serious.

"What is it, honey?" she asked.

He glanced at Candy before saying, "Clint and I aren't the only ones who found our mates while you were gone."

Allison smiled. "Cupid has definitely been working overtime lately." She reached for Cole's hand. "Am I supposed to guess?"

"I don't think you ever would," Cade replied. "It's Matt."

Cole spoke up. "Matt? Now I know I must be dreaming! I had given up on you and Clint ever settling down, but Matt is my idea of a confirmed bachelor."

"She must be very special," Allison said.

"She is, Mom," Cade replied. "We're all eager for you to meet her, but before you do, we'd like to explain something about her background."

Allison glanced at Cole, afraid to guess at the reason for her son's tense expression. "All right," she said, pushing back from the table. "Let's go into the den and you can tell us about the woman who performed a miracle in Matt's life."

Whatever she had been expecting—and now she couldn't remember all the thoughts that had flitted through her head at the time—Cade's news had been so shocking she wasn't certain she would ever forget the moment. It was indelibly etched in her mind—the quiet ticking of the mantel clock, sunlight striping the tiled floor, forming patterns of light and dark, the grave faces of her family watching her. Nor would she ever forget their love and how comforted by it she'd been while Cade told them about Jill Anderson... How she had barged into Matt's office, her outrageous statements, the visit to the ranch and the diary.

The diary.

He'd handed it to her. She remembered how puzzled she was at the time. What did Aunt Letty's diary have to do with her? Cole had taken it and started skimming the pages. It was when he suddenly looked up at Cade and asked, "Does this mean—?" then looked sharply at her that Allison felt it had something to do with her father.

"Does she explain why she fired Dad?" she asked, leaning against Cole's shoulder.

"No. It was written years before that, long before either one of us was born," Cole replied slowly, absently, as he read the rest of the contents. "You'd better look at this," he said, handing the diary to her.

Something slid out of the slim volume and fell into her lap. Allison picked it up curiously. It was a small lock of dark hair, tied with a faded ribbon.

She began to read. By the time she finished tears were rolling unheeded down her cheeks. She finally looked up, seeking Cole's support. "Then this means that— If Aunt Letty had only—"

"Allison, love," Cole said in his low voice, "remember that this happened a long time ago. What you need to focus on now is that the woman Matt loves is part of both of us, don't you see?"

"But Dad never knew. He never guessed that he had a son." She stared down at the faded writing. "He always wanted a son."

"He loved his daughter very much. Never forget that."

"Mother would have been shattered to learn about the baby."

"Yes. The whole family would have been shocked beyond belief," Cole replied. "It's hard to believe, isn't it? Aunt Letty? And your dad?"

Today, as she sat with Janine enjoying the festivities, Allison knew the weeks that had passed since their homecoming had given her time to adjust to what had happened so long ago.

As though she'd been following her thoughts, Janine said, "It's uncanny how much Jill looks like you, Allison. She could be your daughter instead of a niece by marriage."

"Yes." The women smiled at each other in mutual understanding. "Funny how things work out, isn't it? If Dad and Letty had married I would never have been born. Even if I'd been their daughter, I would have been Cole's cousin. Feeling the way I do about him, I believe it would have been painful to love him and know I could never have more than a cousin's relationship with him. It's sad to think about what my dad and Letty must have gone through, but it helps to know that things worked out for all of us in the long run."

"I still consider Jill to be the miracle woman. She managed to get past all of Matt's walls. You know, he and Cam have had several late-night talks since we returned that have brought them even closer together. I can't tell you how pleased I am to see him so happy."

One of Katie's daughters came over with a tray of snacks and a selection of cold drinks. After chatting with her for a few minutes, they were left alone once again.

Janine sighed with contentment. "So now we have another lawyer in the family."

"And another government agent."

"And another artist. The Callaways seem to keep picking the same kind of people."

"We need strong men and women to marry into the family, just to keep all those Callaways in check."

"Isn't that the truth?" The two women laughed heartily, causing their husbands to seek them out in order to discover whatever it was that amused them so much.

Jill finished speaking with another one of her relatives—she'd missed hearing the name—and walked over to where Matt and Emma stood.

"Need any help?" she asked him.

"I don't suppose I could interest you in leaving early, say in the next five minutes?"

She leaned against him, kissing him on the chin. "My brave hero, ready to run away."

"Look, those other guys were just going through their vows to keep us company. I, on the other hand, have just become a brand-new husband and father. I need to get used to the idea."

"And how do you propose to do that?"

"By spending some alone time with you, of course. So what do you say?"

"That's the best offer I've had in a long time, cowboy."

"Good. Let's turn Emma over to Maria. She said to just let her know when we planned to leave and she'd take her into the house."

"Emma probably won't even miss us, if her last visit out here was any indication. We could probably be gone a week or more."

"I don't have a problem with that, but I don't think you could last that long."

She laughed. "You know me very well."

Cameron walked up just then. "I know you're in a hurry and I really don't blame you, but Cole wanted to get the couples together for a family portrait. That way we'll have proof years from now that you really did have a triple wedding here at the ranch."

"Suits me fine, as long as we can do it in the next five minutes," Matt replied firmly.

The three of them moved toward the patio area where a photographer was waiting.

Aurora, Ariel and Aramis looked on from a safe distance.

"What a wonderful sight," Aurora said with a sigh. "I couldn't be more pleased."

Ariel nodded. "There's just something heart-warming about seeing people in love. They glow with happiness."

Aramis spun around in a circle, laughing. "I still can't get over Matt's complete change of heart . . . or rather his releasing of his poor, battered, locked heart. The change in him is astounding.''

''They've all changed,'' Aurora said. ''Haven't you noticed? We have here a firsthand example of love's transforming power.''

''Then it's time for us to report the results of our work,'' Ariel said. ''I suppose they can take care of themselves for a little while without our help.''

So the Callaway clan was left to celebrate the weddings of Clint, Cade and Matt Callaway with the biggest barbecue and wedding reception the county had seen in many years.

*   *   *   *   *

Dear Reader,

This is the forty-fifth book I have written for Silhouette Books and my first single title release. I'm grateful for the opportunity to share my stories about the Callaway clan with you.

Each member of this fictitious family has become very real to me and I find myself rejoicing with them in their happiness and commiserating with them when life gets a little bumpy for them.

I hope they become as real to you and that you find yourself thinking of them later as friends and neighbors who, like the rest of us, are dealing with life as well as they can.

If you'd like to let me know what you think of this book, please write me at P.O. Box 1121, Dripping Springs, TX 78620.

Best wishes,

Annette Broadrick

MILLION DOLLAR SWEEPSTAKES
AND EXTRA BONUS PRIZE DRAWING

by Jackie Merritt

The Fanon family—born and raised in
Big Sky Country...and heading for a wedding!

Meet them in these books from
Silhouette Special Edition® and
Silhouette Desire® beginning with:

MONTANA FEVER
Desire #1014, July 1996

MONTANA PASSION
That Special Woman!
Special Edition #1051, September 1996

And look for more MADE IN MONTANA titles
in 1996 and 1997!

Don't miss these stories of ranching and love
only from Silhouette Books!

Silhouette®

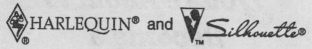
HARLEQUIN® and **Silhouette®**

are proud to present...

HERE COME THE GROOMS™

Four marriage-minded stories written by top Harlequin and Silhouette authors!

Next month, you'll find:

Married?!	by Annette Broadrick
Designs on Love	by Gina Wilkins
It Happened One Night	by Marie Ferrarella
Lazarus Rising	by Anne Stuart

ADDED BONUS! In every edition of *Here Come the Grooms* you'll find $5.00 worth of coupons good for Harlequin and Silhouette products.

On sale at your favorite Harlequin and Silhouette retail outlet.

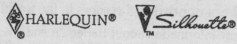
HARLEQUIN®　**Silhouette®**

Look us up on-line at: http://www.romance.net

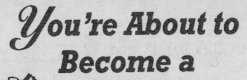